"What The Hell Are You Doing Here?"

His gaze raked over her body, and he tried not to notice how great she looked. But it was useless.

Kate cocked her head and smiled. "You know, Rick, that's what I always loved about you—your warm and friendly greetings."

"Very funny. Now just take those suitcases—" he gestured to the two at her feet "—and go home."

"Not so fast, marine. I have direct orders. If you don't let me take care of you, then you have to go back to the navy hospital. Today."

The last thing he wanted was to have within shouting distance the only woman who could make his blood roar.

Kate lifted the suitcases. "Face it. I'm here for the duration."

Dear Reader,

It's Valentine's Day, time for an evening to remember. Perhaps your perfect night consists of candlelight and a special meal, or a walk along a deserted beach in the moonlight, or a wonderful cuddle beside a fire. My fantasy of what the perfect night entails includes 1) a *very* sexy television actor who starred in a recently canceled WB series 2) a dark, quiet corner in an elegant restaurant 3) a conversation that ends with a daring proposition to… Sorry, some things a girl just has to keep a secret! Whatever your evening to remember entails, here's hoping it's unforgettable.

This month in Silhouette Desire, we also offer you *reads* to remember long into the evening. Kathie DeNosky's *A Rare Sensation* is the second title in DYNASTIES: THE ASHTONS, our compelling continuity set in Napa Valley. Dixie Browning continues her fabulous DIVAS WHO DISH miniseries with *Her Man Upstairs*.

We also have the wonderful Emilie Rose whose *Breathless Passion* will leave you…breathless. In *Out of Uniform*, Amy J. Fetzer presents a wonderful military hero you'll be dreaming about. Margaret Allison is back with an alpha male who has *A Single Demand* for this Cinderella heroine. And welcome Heidi Betts to the Desire lineup with her scintillating surrogacy story, *Bought by a Millionaire*.

Here's to a memorable Valentine's Day…however you choose to enjoy it!

Happy reading,

Melissa Jeglinski

Melissa Jeglinski
Senior Editor
Silhouette Books

Please address questions and book requests to:
Silhouette Reader Service
U.S.: 3010 Walden Ave., P.O. Box 1325, Buffalo, NY 14269
Canadian: P.O. Box 609, Fort Erie, Ont. L2A 5X3

Out of
UNIFORM
AMY J. FETZER

Silhouette®
Desire

Published by Silhouette Books
America's Publisher of Contemporary Romance

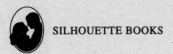 **SILHOUETTE BOOKS**

ISBN 0-373-76636-X

OUT OF UNIFORM

Copyright © 2005 by Amy J. Fetzer

This edition published by arrangement with Harlequin Books S.A.

Visit Silhouette Books at www.eHarlequin.com

Printed in U.S.A.

Books by Amy J. Fetzer

Silhouette Desire

Anybody's Dad #1089
The Unlikely Bodyguard #1132
The Re-Enlisted Groom #1181
Going...Going...Wed! #1265
Wife for Hire #1305
Taming the Beast #1361
Having His Child #1383
Single Father Seeks... #1445
The SEAL's Surprise Baby #1467
Awakening Beauty #1548
Out of Uniform #1636

Silhouette Bombshell

Alias #6

Harlequin Intrigue

Under His Protection #733
Undercover Marriage #799

*Wife, Inc.

AMY J. FETZER

was born in New England and raised all over the world.
She uses her own experiences in creating the characters
and settings for her novels. Married more than twenty
years to a United States Marine and the mother of two
sons, Amy covets the moments when she can curl up
with a cup of cappuccino and a good book.

For my mother-in-law

Leah Catherine Fetzer

For easily dispelling the stigma
that goes with the words "mother-in-law"

For teaching me the art of canning without explosions,
making "sliders" during a winter storm
and for raising terrific sons and daugters…
One in particular

And mostly, Leah, for welcoming me into your family
and teasing me just like I was your own.

I love you

Amy

One

Marines didn't like sitting still. Give them an objective and they'd take it on, grab it by both hands and improvise, adapt and overcome.

Rick's objective was simple. Open a pickle jar. However, his thickly bandaged shoulder and the cast from elbow to knuckles with a half-dozen pins with rubber-stopper tops in his wrist were the obstacles.

A one-armed Marine wasn't overcoming a damn thing. And the possibility that he wouldn't be for a long time left him in a perpetual bad mood. It hadn't let up since he'd been wounded and taken off Force Recon's active list. He wanted back in, wanted his wounds to hurry up and heal so he could get back to his company. Back into action.

But that wasn't getting him pickles.

The simple task had suddenly become like reaching for the Holy Grail. He knew his wounded hand wasn't strong enough to grip the jar. Besides, it hurt like hell and the pins just made it worse. His shoulder was already throbbing, the pain working its way up to his head. He loosened the sling that secured his arm to his side like a straight jacket, and the weight of the cast pulled on his shoulder enough to make him suck in his breath. Determined to get the damn pickles, he tucked the jar under his arm, wedging it against his body, and with his good hand, twisted the cap. The lid popped and liquid spilled down his side and onto the floor.

With a patience he didn't normally have, he removed the sticky jar and set it on the counter, staring at the puddle. He smelled like the mess hall. It was going to take him half an hour just to clean it up. He hated being like this. He'd never been helpless in his life.

He was supposed to be the first man into war, leading his company and taking out a few enemy targets before the battalions landed. Reconnaissance. Not be the invalid. He was glad no one was around to see this.

The doorbell rang.

Great.

Witnesses.

He debated answering it, then after the third chime, tightened the sling and headed to the door. He hoped whoever was on his doorstep would just go the hell away. Since his right arm was locked over his stomach, he had to shift, use his good hand, and the awkwardness reminded him that he couldn't manage the simplest thing without rethinking the process.

He opened the door, already scowling. The last person he expected to see was his estranged wife standing on his porch.

"Hey, handsome."

Kate.

Like the pelting of shrapnel, everything he'd ignored for the last year pinged back into his mind. Attacking him from all sides. His body went into a hard lock-and-load drill, reliving every time he'd touched her, the things they'd done together between the sheets—and everywhere else in this house. Biting waves of longing crashed over him and made him realize how much he'd missed her. That she was still the most beautiful woman he'd ever laid eyes on. Still sexy, vibrant.

And *not* his.

"What the hell are you doing here?"

His gaze raked over her body, and he tried not to

notice how great she looked. But it was useless. He had radar where she was concerned. He took her in like breathing, the way her red hair framed her face and curled like liquid fire over her shoulders to lay over the lush swells of her breasts as if tease him; the way the green shirt set off her eyes and cupped her torso like nobody's business. Did she wear those low-riding cropped pants, and expose her tanned tummy, along with that delectable navel, just to taunt him with what he couldn't have? The discomfort in his jeans went instantly from a twinge to downright painful.

Which just pissed him off. Since he couldn't do anything about it with her anymore.

Kate cocked her head and smiled. "You know, Rick, that's what I always loved about you—your warm friendly greetings."

Smart mouth. "Very funny. Now just take those suitcases—" he gestured to the two at her feet "—and pack your little Irish behind back in your car and go home."

"This is still my home, too."

He stiffened, his eyes narrowing. "No, it's not. Not anymore." Because she'd left him. A year ago she'd told him their marriage was beyond repair and she was tired of being the only one fighting to make it work. The woman didn't know what real fighting was, he thought. And he hadn't seen a damn thing wrong with their marriage.

"Yes, well, I'm not here to rehash our marriage. I'm here to take care of you."

"I don't need it."

"Really?" she said, and he recognized that smug tone. "Is that pickles I smell?" Her gaze lingered for a second on the splatters on his pant leg.

Rick's eyes thinned to slits. "Yes, it is. Now if you'll excuse me…" He started to close the door.

She slapped a hand on the panel and stepped closer. "Not so fast, Marine. I have direct orders."

"Yeah, right."

"If you don't let me take care of you, Rick, then you have to go back to the Navy hospital. Today."

He yanked the door back open, wincing as needles of pain shot up his shoulder to his neck. He wanted to rub it, but the plaster-covered bandages prevented even that simple relief. "Says who? I'm fine alone."

"Your commander and your doctors say so. And oh, here's a stretch—both of them outrank you." She produced a letter and he snatched it, reading it quickly.

"Damn."

"Yes, I knew you'd be just delirious with excitement." She shivered dramatically, then delivered a devious grin that almost made him smile. Almost.

But all he saw was the prospect of having her here, twenty-four–seven. They'd kill each other before the week was out. "Why?"

"Because they both know you as well as I do. You'd

be up, walking around, not taking your medication and trying to tough it out like a hard corps Marine."

"That's my job."

"Not this week, or for the next couple months, at least. And that's *if* you play your cards right and behave."

His gaze thinned. Kate Wyatt knew her husband would rather chew glass than admit he needed anyone. Especially her. "You need help, Rick. I'm a nurse. Since you refused to remain in the hospital, your commander has ordered it." Her gaze moved past him. "And from the looks of the house, well, let's just say that for a man who prides himself on spit and polish—"

"So it's a little messy." Man, that sounded too defensive even to his own ears.

Kate lifted the suitcases. "Back up and let me in. Face it. I'm here for the duration."

He didn't move, debating how to get out of this. The last thing he wanted was having the only woman who could make his blood roar within shouting distance. Hell, his heart was already thumping just looking at her.

"Would you like to read the orders again, *Captain?*" she needled.

Caught between a rock and a command order, Rick knew when to retreat, if only temporarily. Besides, he didn't want the neighborhood getting a load of this. He moved out of the way, sweeping his good arm to welcome her inside. Into a house she'd helped decorate and take care of, then had left.

She passed close in front of him and he caught a whiff of her perfume, felt the heat of her body like a sting. He ground his teeth, resisting the urge to lean closer and inhale the scent that was all Kate. All woman.

All hot, ripe body and great smiles.

Man, seeing her shouldn't be this hard.

When he went to take her bags, she backed up and snapped, "No, you're not to use that arm at all if you want to be fit for Force Recon again. And that includes both arms."

"I can use this arm fine." He wiggled his fingers, then flapped his left elbow.

"The muscles are connected, Rick, and straining your good side in deference to your wound will mean you just take longer to recover. And look a little lopsided, too," she teased, swinging her arm like a monkey. He wasn't amused. "Is that what you want?" He let his hand fall away. She dragged the heavy suitcases farther inside, then, leaving one, took the other to the guest room.

Rick didn't move while she carted off the second, and he felt very unchivalrous just standing there.

Hell, he felt like a five-year-old—and lucky he was dressed.

When Kate came back, she stopped in front of him. "You look tired." He wore a T-shirt with one sleeve cut out so he could get it around the cast and thick bandages. All it did was stretch the fabric tight across his bulging chest muscles. The couple days' growth of beard only added to his rugged do-or-die appearance, which she'd fallen madly in love with four years ago.

"I'm annoyed," he said pointedly. "And I feel fine." But he wasn't. He rubbed his jaw, ignoring the pain throbbing steadily in his shoulder. The cast felt tighter, but he'd be damned if he'd let her see he wanted to curl up in a ball and whimper like a swabbie.

"When did you last take your medication?"

He didn't respond, and Kate had her answer.

"Rick," she groaned. "It's to fight infection from the surgery, jarhead." She went to the kitchen, slipping on the pickle juice and grabbing the counter.

She met his gaze. "I see we've had an accident."

"I swear if you talk to me like you do your patients—" he pointed at her, the twinkle in her eyes irritating him even more "—I'll throw you in a closet and never let you out."

She hid a smile and muttered, "Sorry."

She took inventory of the bottles of pills on the counter, read the labels and then dispensed them onto the counter with such efficiency Rick *felt* like one of the faceless people in the hospital. Which was why he'd chosen to return home and sleep in his own bed.

And now had his very own soon-to-be-ex wife stand-ing in the sticky kitchen, looking like she had in his dreams.

Hell, she was always in his dreams, but dreams didn't account for much in his book. They were fan-tasy. She needed to look more like a nurse, he groused silently. Because with every ripe, well-defined inch of her packed into that cute outfit, she was sending his imagination down the road to ruin. And she'd been here, what—two minutes?

She handed him his antibiotic pill, then a glass of water, standing guard as he took it. Satisfied, she went to a drawer, pulled out a notepad and pen and jotted down the time, date and dosage. That she remembered where the pad was and that he hadn't changed the location of anything in the house said something to him—he was clinging to something he didn't have anymore. A wife. Someone who loved him.

But she'd left him, and the old resentment rose in him.

She dispensed a painkiller next, holding it out to him. He didn't take it.

"You're in pain."

"I'm fine." Great. Was that all he could say in his own defense?

Her voice went liquid soft. "Rick, you had major surgery less than a week ago, and already this morn-ing you're perspiring." She touched his cheek. Her hand was so cool on his face, he nearly moaned. "Take this and go to bed."

If you come with me, an inner voice shouted. He grabbed the pill and, like a child, jammed it in his mouth. "I'm going to watch the game."

"That's fine, as long as you get off your feet and rest." Kate went for the mop and bucket as he walked out of the kitchen. When he was out of sight, she sagged against the counter, fighting tears.

Oh, it was so hard seeing him like this. He was barely standing on his feet. Dark circles made his blue eyes look hollow, and his skin had lost some of its usual tan. Other than that, he looked pretty good for a man who'd been wounded enough to need a couple of blood transfusions.

He had no idea how difficult it had been for her to stay away this long. Or that she hadn't.

She'd been working for her civilian doctor when Rick's commanding officer had called her. Hearing the words *he's been shot* had shattered everything inside her. They'd stabilized him in a field hospital and then airlifted him from somewhere in the Middle East to an Air Force base in Germany for surgery.

Kate had been on a flight within an hour. She'd sat outside the OR during the surgery and was by his bedside for two days until he was off the critical list. He'd been too deep under with morphine to know she was even there, and she'd made the staff swear not to tell him. He wouldn't want her to see him like that. But watching him lie in the hospital bed hooked up to IVs, a monitor beeping out his heartbeat, and bandaged from throat to fingertips…all she could do was thank God he was alive. And realize that she'd never stopped loving him.

Not living with him anymore hadn't lessened the worry. Because she still *felt* married, felt connected to him, she thought, pushing away from the counter and grabbing the mop.

She'd handled having him walk out their door and into danger for years during their marriage. She even understood that he could never talk about the missions; there were some things wives and the American public didn't need to know. So she'd kept her worry capped, not wanting to be a distraction for him while he was on the battlefield, but it wore on them because Rick would never open up to her. About anything. Not even his feelings for her.

That was the reason she'd left. She'd been doing all the work, all the talking. And that shield of his made her doubt his love for her. Or if he even needed her in his life.

She rubbed her face. Why was she analyzing this again?

If he'd wanted her to stay, he would have fought harder for her. He'd have picked up the phone at least once and asked her to come back, to try to work it out.

But his pride was too big and his heart too tightly sealed.

That hurt the most.

He'd fight for his country, die for it. But when it came to her and their marriage, he just let her walk out the door without a word.

That was the last time she'd seen him until he was on a gurney being wheeled into the O.R. by two Corpsmen.

Still exhausted from the long flights and jet lag, Kate battled with the memory as she finished cleaning the floor, then went to the guest room to unpack her things. It felt strange to be back in this house. She struggled for focus, reminding herself this was a job. In-home care. The navy was paying her. She had to get Rick back in fighting form so he could return to what he really loved.

She wandered through the house, straightening up and gathering laundry he'd left in some of the strangest places. Then she made the mistake of walking into their bedroom.

His bedroom, she reminded herself. A wave of longing hit her, making her grip the door jamb. They'd expressed so much love in this room. She looked around at the rich eggplant-and-taupe decor of the room, at the grand four-poster Rice bed they'd picked out a week before the wedding. As he'd paid for it, Rick had whispered that he was going to make love to her every way imaginable in it. Her heart clenched with something close to pain as her body remembered he'd made good on that promise. She touched the tall mahogany post, leaning into it.

The bed was haphazardly made, but it was the matching dresser she noticed instantly. There was nothing on it—none of his things—and after investigating, she learned the drawers were empty. Why didn't he use it? She went to the closet. One half was filled with pressed uniforms, from his evening mess dress to his "jungles," the camouflage utilities he wore in the field. His combat boots were in perfect alignment, varying colors from his black jump boots to buff desert suede. His covers were aligned on the top shelf. His "civvies" filled the rest of the closet, equally as neat as a wall locker in a barracks.

While they were married he'd stored his many uniforms in the guest room closet so she had some space. Except for moving them in here, he'd changed nothing. It was as if he didn't want to acknowledge that she was gone.

Well, she *was* gone. She had a new life, an apartment, she thought, almost angrily stripping the bed, replacing the sheets with fresh. She dusted the room before heading to the garage to start a load of laundry, frowning at the new woodworking tools and chunks of wood on the workbench. Must be house repair stuff.

Satisfied she had a jump on the disorder, she fixed

Rick a sandwich and brought it to him. He was slumped on the sofa, asleep, the remote control in his hand, the TV stuck on a news channel. She set the sandwich down on the side table and drew a blanket over him, then checked his pulse. On a whim she sat on the edge of the sofa by his hip. Reaching out, she grazed his face with her fingers, pushing his short, dark hair off his brow and noticing the cut near his hairline before sweeping her palm over his whiskered jaw. Unconsciously, he turned his face into her hand.

Her heart skipped a couple of beats. He didn't have to say a thing and she was already coming apart inside, as if she were falling under his spell all over again. His quiet strength had first attracted her, then his smile. It changed his whole appearance and always made her stomach do a little flip. He'd done everything right— nothing mushy, just straightforward love that showed in the way he looked at her, the way he touched her body and reached into her soul.

She missed that. The little sparkle, the devilish teasing that overflowed with raw sexuality. Unwisely, she let her gaze run over his body; so sculpted and hard, the thin T-shirt ridged over his six-pack abs. She didn't have to see more—every solid muscled inch of him was imprinted in her mind and invaded her dreams.

Her gaze moved to the pins in his wrist, and for his sake, she hoped his shattered bones healed. If he couldn't function with a weapon, he'd be medically discharged. It would destroy him. The Marine Corps was his life. His entire life.

If the Corps wanted Marines to have a wife, they'd have issued them one. She'd heard that a thousand times from male Marines—most of them married. It was their way of not letting the fact that they had someone at home waiting and worrying get to them when they were in the field. It ticked her off sometimes, too. She'd been as much a part of the Marine Corps family as any Marine. Honestly, the toughest job in the Corps was being a Marine's wife and watching him walk so willingly into danger.

She studied Rick now, her throat closing over a hard lump that hadn't left since she'd learned he'd been wounded. She didn't want him to see her crying over this. He'd shrug it off, tell her he was fine, no big deal. But just the same, she wondered what it was like to take a bullet. To know that you might not make it home. *And that home was empty,* a voice in her head screamed.

I know, I know. But I tried.

When she'd married him she'd known he wasn't the kind of man who talked a lot about himself, or his feelings, and she didn't set out to change him. She'd hoped that he'd feel secure enough that he would at least not shut her out, and would perhaps turn to her when he was hurting. But not Rick. Even when he'd lost one of his men in combat, he still hadn't confided in her.

He'd barely spoken at all. Instead, he had gone out in the backyard and chopped wood for two days, gotten drunk with his buddies. Afterward, he was back to the same man she'd always loved.

She swore sometimes that when he was hurting, he moved on autopilot.

Heck, he never even told her when he wanted her. He'd just pull her into his arms, kiss her, and that was it.

Well, she thought, smiling, that hadn't been *it*—sex had always been so exciting between them. She missed it. But she needed words. It was so female, she admitted. So girlie to need it, but she couldn't get around the fact that the last time she'd heard him say he loved her was when he said his wedding vows. She needed to feel as if she meant as much to him as his military career.

Duty is to God, country and Corps. Everything else is just gravy, Marines said.

Kate didn't want to be gravy—she needed to know she was equally important to him. But when he didn't fight for her, she understood she wasn't.

Damn him.

Just be his nurse, she told herself resolutely, laying her hand on his chest and feeling him breathe, absently counting off the times while she looked at her watch. When she looked up, his eyes were open.

His lips curved in a sleepy smile that was too sexy

for his own good. Her heart tripped all over itself to catch up with the lost beats.

"Hi, baby," he murmured groggily.

Her heart clenched hard. "Hey yourself, handsome."

A year fell away, a year of being alone without him in her life, in her bed. Kate's eyes burned. And when his good hand moved up her back, a familiar heat slid over her skin, awakening her.

"So, is this what it takes to get you back here?"

It would have taken so little, she mused. One phone call. "You're telling me you got wounded just so I'd come be your nurse?"

His lips quirked. "I've done dumber things for you."

"Yeah, sure. When?"

"How 'bout the time I wore that stupid underwear for you?"

"But you looked *so* sexy in it." Just the memory made her heart pound.

"Glad you were the only one who saw it. Imagine the ribbing I'd have suffered if my teams knew I wore a gold thong for you."

"It's called a slingshot, and you don't wear any underwear except when you're in uniform, anyway." That had always turned her on.

He gave her a devilish look. "I'm not wearing any now." He applied pressure to her back, drawing her near.

She didn't know what made her say it. "Funny, neither am I."

Rick groaned and pulled her closer, laying his mouth over hers. Their first contact in a year was electric, the rawness of desire spiraling out of control. In seconds, he was devouring her.

"Oh, man," he murmured, and kissed her hungrily.

Kate sank into it, her body screaming recognition as his mouth made a slow, luxurious slide over hers. His tongue, dipping and sweeping made her spine tingle with a pulse of need that wrapped around her and settled between her thighs. His free hand swept her spine to her breast, cupping it, his fingertips making slow erotic circles over her nipple. Fire radiated, her response consuming her and pouring into him. His kiss grew stronger, raw and devouring, then he tried to draw his bound arm around her, and flinched, growling in pain.

She lurched back as he grabbed his shoulder.

"Dammit," he muttered.

Kate shot to her feet, guilt pinging through her. "It's just as well. We shouldn't have done that, and I didn't come here to pick up anything, Rick. I came here to help you recuperate."

"Well then, be a damn nurse and stay away from me!" he snapped angrily. "You might have called it quits on us, but that doesn't mean I *ever* stopped wanting you!"

Wanting her? Not needing, loving? She couldn't allow herself more than nursing him back to health. He wouldn't change, and he'd break her heart once more. She couldn't live through that. Not again. She'd never survive. She'd already lost something more precious than her marriage, and she was barely surviving now.

"You're just horny," she said tightly. "Don't confuse lust with anything remotely resembling actually *needing* me, Rick." She spun around and headed for the kitchen, her body still stinging with desire and her hurt burning her throat.

Two

Rick felt like a prisoner in an enemy camp.

The only problem was he knew he couldn't make an escape. And the camp commander was like a demon on wheels.

From his "cell" on the sofa, Rick watched Kate move around the house with military efficiency, cleaning, rearranging things back to some semblance of order. His uniforms and gear might be able to pass inspection at any given moment, but when it came to dust bunnies, Rick had his priorities.

Since her last remark, she'd moved around him as if he wasn't there, and Rick savored the small pleasure of simply watching her. She was graceful, so feminine and curvy in all the right places. She had a gorgeous hourglass figure like a movie star, and he knew when he held her he held a woman—round, soft, sweet smelling. His body sat up and took notice, which wasn't surprising. He'd always had a perpetual hard-on around his wife.

But she wasn't his wife now.

Somewhere in the legal system there were separation papers saying just that. His brow knit as he remembered her call, telling him it was best if they ended it. He hadn't pleaded with her to come back, though he'd wanted to beg. He'd figured if she'd talked to a lawyer, her mind was made up and there was no changing it.

That said a lot to a guy.

Old anger festered, resentment stewing in him, and though he itched to pull her into his lap as she passed close, he distracted himself with flipping through channels for something more interesting.

It wasn't happening.

"Rick, that's annoying. Pick something," she said as she passed. Watching her go just reminded him of all the good times they'd had, how much he'd loved her and how easily she'd left. There wasn't anything wrong with their marriage that he could point a finger at—except that she always wanted him to tell her what he was *feeling*.

Rick wasn't a sharing kind of guy, unless he was furious with someone. He'd been raised by people who didn't give a damn if he was hurting, having been passed from foster home to foster home, then to an unfeeling uncle who'd told him to deal with it. So he did. Alone. He'd let his guard down once, and the lousy reception he got was enough to make certain he didn't do it again. He considered feelings a weakness, and he didn't need to get "in touch" with any part of himself. He knew what kind of man he was, and was content with working things out on his own. Why couldn't Kate understand that?

Why couldn't she see that he didn't want her to experience the burdens and, sometimes, the ugliness he had?

Her last comment played through his mind again, and frowning, Rick left the sofa and headed into the kitchen. She was filling the dishwasher with the sinkful of dishes he'd left behind. He didn't want her cleaning up after him, taking care of him. He wanted her sweet little ass out of this house, so he'd be left alone.

"What was that last crack about?" he demanded.

Kate glanced over her shoulder, confused for a second. "It wasn't a crack. It was…insight. Don't confuse wanting sex with actually needing me."

"I've always needed you."

Her heart clenched a little. "You've wanted me. In your bed, in this house. But you don't really need me."

"I say again, woman, what does that mean?"

Woman? She knew he was mad when he said that.

She threw the dishrag in the sink and walked up to him. "It means you survived quite well without me for nearly a year, and now that you're injured, you need help. I'm here to give it. But that's where it has to stay. Nurse to patient. Because it's obvious you still aren't willing to open up to me." And let me into your heart. Deep in.

"Kate, baby, I loved you."

She arched a brow. "Past tense?" The sting of that nearly made her legs crumble.

"What the hell do you expect? You left *me*." The humiliation of that failure was enough to make him grind his teeth.

"Because you wouldn't talk to me, Rick. You keep everything locked up so tight I don't think *you* even know what you feel."

"Dammit, what do you want from me? To tell you I miss you? I do. That I want you? Like crazy. But don't tell me you're here for any reason other than you feel sorry for me."

She blinked and reared back. "Pity? For you? A man who can hold his breath underwater for two minutes? Who jumps out of airplanes into heavy combat because it's the quickest way into the front lines of battle? A man who survived a week in the Iraqi desert, alone, with a K-bar knife and a canteen? No, I don't feel sorry for you in the least."

"Then why are you really here?"

She hated that his voice went soft and tender; she wanted to stay mad. "You love the Marines, and I'm here to see that you get back to what you love most, as soon as you can and in the best shape possible. Because that will make you happy." *Even if it's without me.*

"Okay, I can buy that," he said after a moment.

Were all men that clueless? "Good. Are we done jabbing?"

"I doubt it."

She made a frustrated sound as she turned away and left the kitchen. He followed her to the bathroom and watched her gather his shaving supplies.

"You need a shave," she said, noticing his frown.

"I shave when I shower, you know that. Or have you forgotten everything?"

An image pierced her anger, of her shaving him in the shower before they'd made love against the wall like wild, hungry teenagers. She closed her eyes for a second, the frantic pulse of the memory shooting through her body like a rocket.

"No, I haven't." *Not a single moment.*

He moved closer, hemming her in, his towering strength nearly smothering her. "Me, either," he said, his voice a husky growl that make her skin tingle.

Unable to help it, she reached out and touched his jaw. "So do you want to bathe and shave? Or is that cowboy stubble a new look for you?"

"Hell no, makes my face itch. But I have to do it

left-handed because of this." He knocked on the cast. "I'll turn my face into hamburger."

"Lucky for you I'm here, then. I have something that will help."

She brushed past him out the door, and a couple seconds later was back with a cellophane wrapped hospital pack. Breaking it open, she flipped out a plastic sleeve.

"This goes over your hand and shoulder and will create suction on your skin, so water won't get in."

He was relieved. "Outstanding. I didn't think a plastic bag was going to keep this thing very dry for long."

"If you were in the hospital, they'd have helped you shower with this."

"I don't need help to take a damn bath."

Her expression told him he was pushing his luck. "Stop fighting me, Rick." Then she looked him in dead in the eye and ordered, "Strip."

Rick stared at her for a second, thinking she was trying hard to be impersonal now. *We'll see.* Not bothering to struggle with the T-shirt, he grabbed a handful of the front and yanked. The garment tore from his body with one pull. He dropped it to the floor.

Rick, taut and tight with pounds of rippling muscle, was about as good as it got, Kate thought, wanting to be wearing nothing but her skin, and pressing it against him.

"It will make a good rag," she said blandly, and

knelt, untying his sneakers and removing them. When she glanced up, she found him staring down at her with a hooded look. Then he pulled at his belt buckle, jerked it open and unzipped his pants. Kate stood abruptly, and the hint of a dark, sexy smile curved his lips. Her toes practically curled. He was teasing her, knowing she was a sucker for his body.

Not one to pass up an opportunity, Rick gripped her hip, pulling her closer, and when her hands splayed over his chest, he felt seared all the way to his spine.

"Didn't we just discuss this?" Kate said, feeling the length of his arousal between them. "Or are you still that hardheaded?"

Scowling, he let her go. "Apparently."

She moved around him and turned on the bathwater.

"No, a shower."

"No," she said patiently. "You won't have the balance on a wet floor. This has a rail on the wall at least. And it will do your muscles good to have some heat on them. I'm betting your shoulder and arm isn't all that hurts." The bruises on his spine were still discolored and ugly. She sat on the edge of the tub, testing the water, adding a packet of something from the hospital stuff she'd brought.

"Epsom salts," she said, swishing it around. "If you have any cuts it might sting a little, but it will feel great."

You in that tub with me would take the sting away,

he thought, then cursed when his groin thickened. He was going to be a blathering idiot by the end of the day.

"Leave me alone, Kate. I can manage."

"Really? Try." She handed him the protective sleeve and watched him struggle to get it over the pins. When he sucked in his breath, she took it and gently worked the plastic sleeve over his hand and up his shoulder. She pressed on it tightly and it adhered to his skin.

"Okay now, git." He wasn't about to let this humiliation go on with her watching.

She ignored him, taping the open edge for extra protection. "You could slip."

"Then I fall."

"And it will set you back a month. Is that what you want?" She pressed the last piece of tape in place.

That was the second time she'd asked that, Rick realized, frowning. She looked up at him, hands on her trim hips. Hell, if she was going to be a pest... He tugged his trousers farther open and let them drop to the floor. His eyes almost dared her to inspect him as he stepped out of them.

Instead, Kate swallowed, avoiding a glance at everything he owned. But standing in the bathroom with her handsome, naked, soon-to-be-ex husband was something she hadn't really considered when she'd agreed to this. Oh, he could really do some damage to her protective armor if he kept this up.

When he climbed into the tub, the intense urge to

pat his tight behind nearly overpowered her. He groaned as he sank into the hot water. The tub was custom made because he was so tall and he'd wanted it to accommodate both of them. It reminded her that their marriage had included a lot of sex and very little deep verbal communication.

He braced his injured arm on the edge and let the other sink under the cloudy water. Kate pulled a stool close, laying out bath items, then leaned over to gently lift his head and cushion his neck with a rolled towel.

Rick closed his eyes, tempted to nip at her skin, since she was pushing her breasts in his face, but instead sank deeper into the water. "Thanks. Man, this feels great."

"Soak for a bit. I'll be back in a few minutes."

"Running off so soon?" he challenged.

Already at the door, she turned back to look at him. The water was above his waist and cloudy white, but did nothing to hide what lay beneath. "I'm not running anywhere. I thought you'd like privacy." She sure as heck needed it.

"You could wash my back?" He grinned.

Her heart did a quick tumble in her chest to see him smile. "There is a back brush beside you."

Rick snatched up the soap. She was acting damn impersonal for a woman who'd made incredibly erotic love to her patient for years. Left alone, he tried lathering up the washcloth with soap but couldn't manage the simple task. The harder he struggled, the more he ended up chasing the bar around the tub. It reminded him that he was a nonfunctioning Marine.

Useless.

Hell, he'd like nothing more than to pull Kate onto his lap, but couldn't do anything about it once he got her there. He stared at the soap and washcloth, then clamped the cloth between his knees and rubbed it with the bar. Eventually, he managed to scrub himself, and satisfied he was decently clean, he reached for the shampoo.

Kate stood outside the bathroom, hearing him curse, ready to pop in and help whether he wanted it or not. He could tease her all he wanted, but it just made her heart feel bruised. Giving in to him would accomplish nothing except a little temporary satisfaction. Good satisfaction, but still temporary. Like picking up the best parts of their life and not dealing with the bad.

Well, it wasn't *so* bad, she thought. Much of it had been great. Until she'd started feeling as if she were an appendage to his life, and not really in it. She didn't have any foolish dreams of getting him to share himself with her this time.

She heard a thump and looked in. Seeing him struggle to reach the shampoo bottle, she stepped inside.

When he looked up, it was to glare at her as if his inability was her fault. She ignored it, used to that kind of frustration from patients, and sat on the stool.

Taking the shampoo, she lathered his hair and rubbed his scalp, avoiding the cut on his hairline. He moaned like a tired bear. She smiled, remembering when they'd shared this tub, how he liked conditioning her hair because it made his hands so slick they skated over her body. He had great hands, knew all the right places to stroke and tease until she was quivering and begging him to push inside her—

Abruptly, she picked up the hand-held sprayer and rinsed his hair, wanting to douse herself. He tipped his head back, letting the water cascade over his face.

Then those deep blue eyes zeroed in on her, making her insides spring apart for the hundredth time that day.

It felt like Chinese water torture to Rick. A beautiful woman—one he'd explored thoroughly for years—was treating him like a patient, and he was so hard for her right now, he could crack walnuts. He tossed down the washcloth strategically so she wouldn't notice.

Fat chance.

His gaze lowered. "You're wet."

She looked down. Her shirt was soaked, her nipples straining against the wet cloth. When he started to reach for her, she slapped the razor into his open hand. He clutched it, and she filled her palm with shaving

cream. She knew him; he'd have to try shaving himself before asking for help.

"Kate," he warned.

"Oh, for pity's sake, this is getting old. I swear,
I've never heard you gripe as much as you have in the
last couple hours. Why struggle when you don't have
to?" She lathered his face.

"It makes me feel like a child."

She let her gaze slide up and down all the man and
muscle exposed, then simply arched a brow. "You
mean there's a sweet infantile innocence in there somewhere?"

He snarled something under his breath and she held
up a mirror for him, watching him scrape away a couple days' worth of beard. His gaze flicked up, catching hers. She was inches from him.

All Rick had to do was lean in a bit to kiss her. Yet
he kept shaving, and when he couldn't adequately
reach one side with his left hand, she took the razor.

She shaved him carefully, smoothing her fingers
over his skin to be certain she got all the bristles. She
cupped water, rinsing, sliding her thumb over his chin,
around his lips. He nipped her fingertip, his flashing
eyes meeting hers, and Kate experienced the power
this man had over her. He sucked the tip for a second,
and she hesitated, wanting his mouth on hers, wanting every part of him connecting to her. Right now.
When the back of his knuckles grazed her breast, a bolt

of hot need slammed through her. She jerked back, blinking.

Oh, for pity's sake. If he kept this up she'd be on the floor spread-eagle, begging him to take her.

"We're done. You need to stand," she said coolly, grabbing the hand sprayer.

Angered at her indifference, he snarled, "Dammit, Kate, get the hell out of here! I'm not completely helpless."

She tossed down the sprayer and stood. "Call me when you want the sleeve off."

"I can do that."

"No, you can't. I taped it on, *Captain.*" She stormed out.

Using the rail for balance, Rick stood slowly, rinsed himself, then stepped out and reached for a towel. He dried off and was struggling to wrap the towel around his waist when she walked back in. He glared at her as, with a flat expression, she strode up to him and adjusted the terry cloth. Her fingers grazed his groin and it jumped to life again as she tucked the towel tight.

Damn thing had a mind of its own, he thought a second before she yanked off the tape in one shot.

He winced. "You liked that too much."

"Yes, of course. I so enjoy seeing you torn, bleeding and in pain."

Her voice fractured a tiny bit, and Rick wanted to kick himself. Kate was not a vindictive person. There wasn't a mean bone in her beautiful body. It was the reason he'd never confided in her about some of the things he'd done. She wasn't strong enough to hear it. She would turn away. *And what did* not *telling her leave you?* a voice asked. *Except alone?*

She removed the sleeve and draped it over the shower stall, then gathered up the debris. "There are fresh clothes on your bed in your room."

Your bed, *your* room, he thought, remembering when it was "ours."

She left him alone, and Rick decided this had to end. He couldn't take her being here without touching her, without wanting to be inside her and feel her grip him, hear the delicious little sounds she made just before she climaxed in his arms.

God, he wanted his wife. Bad.

And all he got was Florence Nightingale in tight pants.

Dressed in sweatpants and a T-shirt Kate had cut the arm out of, Rick sat on the edge of the bed. She was out there somewhere fussing over something, thinking she was helping when she was just driving him closer to insanity.

Checking his watch, he grabbed the phone and dialed, asking for his battalion executive officer. His C.O. was still with the battalion overseas, but the X.O. had come back with the advanced party to set up the battalion again.

"Sir. I have to inquire, is this nurse necessary?"

"Yes. I've spoken to your surgeon. He let you go home with the express condition that you return to the hospital every two days for a checkup. You missed it, which was a direct order, Marine." Rick winced. Though he'd called, the fact that he'd fallen asleep facedown in his bed for an entire day wasn't excuse enough. "So Dr. Fisher contacted me."

"I don't need a nurse, sir."

"I would think, son, that a pretty woman caring for you would be better than a corpsman in combat boots."

Kate's image burst in his mind, and Rick glanced toward the door. Somewhere in the kitchen, she was clanging pots. Frustrated and annoyed. "Yes, sir. Roger that, sir."

"The fact that it's your wife—"

"Begging the Major's pardon, sir, but she's my ex-wife."

"Not according to the Marine Corps and this state. Not yet. Is that something you can't handle, Captain? She took leave from her job to fill in, at Dr. Fisher's request. The Navy didn't have any nurses to spare."

Rick didn't want any of the troops or their families neglected because hospital personnel were leaving their positions to come check on his sorry butt.

"Recuperate, Captain. We need you back in fighting form."

"Yes, sir."

"And Captain?"

"Sir?"

"Maybe you should take advantage of this opportunity?"

Rick couldn't stop his smile. "You don't know my wife, sir."

"Apparently, Marine, neither do you."

With that, the Major hung up. Rick stared at the receiver, then put the phone back in the cradle.

A pot clanged, dishes chimed.

Yup, he thought, *I'm in the enemy camp with no reinforcements in sight.*

Three

When Rick entered the kitchen, she was prowling through the cabinets, the freezer and fridge, the air punctuated with the snap of cupboard doors and a whole lot of muttering.

"What *are* you doing?"

"Looking for something to cook! Do you know you have only a six-pack of beer, one egg and a jar of pickles in there?" She pointed to the fridge.

His brows shot up. "There's beer?" He crossed the kitchen.

She barricaded the refrigerator door. "Not with painkillers, you don't."

"Kate…" he warned, reaching around her.

She shifted her hip, cutting off his approach. "It'll raise your blood pressure."

She was raising his blood pressure, he thought, and had images of backing her up against the nearest counter and kissing her till she melted.

"When you no longer take them, you can have a beer."

Rick pushed his fingers through his hair. "Jeez, you're a tyrant." Her chin tipped up and he wanted to nibble on it, and keep going—all the way down to the curve in her hip where she was ticklish.

"There isn't any chow," he said patiently, "because I've been deployed for over five months."

"Oh." She knew that, Kate told herself. She'd known exactly where he was, even if she wasn't here. "Well, then it's take-out, I guess."

"I have some MREs in my gear locker."

She made a face. Field rations? "Meals Ready to Eat? Yuck."

He pointed to the bottom drawer near the stove. "Take-out menus are in there."

She opened the drawer and grabbed a handful, sifting. "Pizza, Chinese, Thai, Mexican, sea food?"

"T & W has the best fried oysters in the state."

She glanced at him, arching a brow. "Oh, really?"

"Yeah, I have a standing order." He said it just because he knew it would tick her off. She was too practical to have take-out unless it was a special occasion.

He'd been eating it since she'd left. He could have gone to the mess hall, but he didn't want anyone knowing about his private life. A company commander eating alone in the mess hall would open up too many doors to gossip.

She ordered Chinese, and by the time it was delivered, she had the table set. He was used to eating it right out of the carton, but then, he'd bet she knew that already.

"I'll grocery shop in the morning."

"There's cash over there." He nodded toward the ceramic jar on the counter.

She didn't look, knowing the pretty little tulip-shaped jar was where she'd kept her "house cash." "Want anything special?" she asked.

"Anything would be great, Kate. But I wonder…is cooking in your job description?"

She made a face at him, spearing her chicken and cashew nuts. "If MREs are the option, it is."

"They taste like heaven in the field. If anything, just to wash away the taste of dust."

"Where were you on deployment?"

He hesitated, then jabbed a piece of food with his fork. "Afghanistan."

Her breath rushed in.

He didn't look up. "I can't tell you any more, Kate, you know that."

"Well, now I know why all the plants are dead."

He glanced at a fern that was so brittle a slight wind would make it disintegrate.

"Why didn't you ask Candice next door to water them for you? I'm sure she would have."

He simply shrugged and Kate studied him.

"You didn't tell anyone I wasn't here, did you?"

"Not anyone's business."

"Not even Jace?" Jace was a lieutenant, Rick's company executive officer. And his friend.

Carefully, he set his fork down, wiped his mouth with a napkin and looked up. "No. Not even him. But they aren't stupid. When you weren't there when I left on the plane, I think they figured something was up."

Kate's face reddened. He'd left for war, and she hadn't been there to see him off.

Rick sensed her pity, and hated it. "They asked. As far as I was concerned the subject was off-limits."

Well, that didn't surprise her. "I see," she muttered, and if she could feel worse, she did. She'd thought about the position she'd put him in many times over the last few months. The Marine Corps was a tightly knit group. They took care of their own. And when it came to gossip, discretion was not the better part of valor.

"It wouldn't have mattered," he said.

"How so?"

"Because *I* still don't get why you left."

Her head jerked up. "Then we really haven't progressed, have we?"

"How about you tell me why you felt the need to walk out on our marriage?"

Why didn't you come after me? she wanted to snap, but said, "I did, Rick, a thousand times. You won't share anything with me."

He made a snide sound. "We talked all the time."

"Sure, we did. About average stuff, what to do on the weekend, what flowers to plant, but I never heard what was in your heart. I don't even know that much about your past."

His features tightened. "It's not as nice as yours. Let's leave it at that."

"Oh, for the love of Mike, this is what I mean. You know, I can even count how many times I've heard you say you loved me!"

I do, she wanted to hear. *I do love you.* But he said nothing, staring. Fuming. He hadn't said how he felt when she'd left, any more than he'd missed her.

"Every time I thought we were finally communicating, that you'd open up and be comfortable enough to share more than the mundane, you'd be off on a deployment and we'd be right back where we were."

"Which was?"

"Not being close enough for two people who planned on spending the rest of their lives together."

"Well, that's not the case now, is it?" He stood, shoving in the chair and picking up his plate. "We aren't sharing our lives anymore, Kate, because *you* split."

He didn't love her enough to stop her. He hadn't even tried, dammit. It would have taken so little, she thought, her eyes tearing up. One call. *Anything.*

"I may have left, Rick Wyatt, but you know what?"

"I'm sure you'll tell me," he snapped, then noticed the tears in her eyes.

"You didn't do a damn thing to stop me." She rushed from the room.

Rick dropped his head forward, exhaling a long, tired breath. He hated himself for making her cry, and she was right, dammit.

He rubbed his face, then drove his fingers through his short hair. If this kept up, it was going to be a long and difficult recovery. And by the end, they'd be shredded.

At three in the morning, Rick stood outside the guest room, watching Kate sleep. If his shoulder wasn't throbbing he'd still be asleep right now.

It felt natural to go find her. How could he resist when she was this close again? She looked like a wood sprite curled on her side, her red hair spread over the pillow. The room was filled with her fragrance, and he stepped inside, lowering himself into the padded chair near the foot of the bed.

It felt familiar, watching her sleep. When they'd first married, he'd lain awake sometimes for hours just staring at her, thinking he was the luckiest man on the planet that she'd fallen in love with him. The day he'd married her he'd thought he'd finally have what he'd dreamed about as a kid.

Someone to love him. Someone who needed him.

He'd grown up without love, and for a while, he'd given up looking for it. Sure, foster parents liked him well enough, but that wasn't the same as when Kate stared into his eyes and he knew she loved only him.

Rick rubbed his face, wondering how everything had gone so wrong, and what he'd done to cause it. It had to be him, he thought. Kate was a man's dream in a wife. A great wife for a Marine, too. She knew damn near every individual in his company by name, plus their families. She'd had the wives over for coffee, checked on the young troops' families when they were deployed.

She'd made Rick look good.

The best thing to happen to him in his life was right now lying in a bed ten feet away, and somehow, he'd let her slip through his fingers. He wanted to grab her back, keep her.

She stirred, shifting from her side to her back. Her thin nightgown strap slid off her shoulder, exposing the lush round curves of her breasts. Like a moth to a flame, he was drawn, moving to her bedside and staring down at her. Moonlight from the window streamed across her body, and his heart ached for her.

Just plain *ached*.

He wanted to crawl in there with her, feel her against him, feel whole again. He'd tried to tell himself he didn't need anyone, but he needed Kate. She'd been the only anchor in a very lonely life. The last year was proof enough. He'd felt lost until he opened the door this morning.

As he stared down at her, a hundred thoughts marched through his brain, torturing him. Good grief, he didn't even know where she lived! Had she dated anyone in the last year? Was she in love with another man? Did whoever it was touch her? The thought of another man putting his hands on her made Rick's stomach tighten, his heart constrict. She was his!

Face it, Marine. You lost her. You screwed up and lost her.

Yet here she was. When he needed her, she'd come running, wanting to take care of him, but not wanting to love him again.

It killed him to know that.

And he was tired of dying a little each day.

He turned away, stopping long enough to grab a painkiller, then headed back to their bed. Alone.

Showered and dressed before dawn, Kate grabbed the copy of Rick's chart and headed for the master bedroom to check in on him. Her brows shot up when she found his bed empty, and she hurried through the house, searching for him.

A little needle of panic shot through her when she couldn't find him.

She stood in the kitchen and shouted, "Rick! Where are you?"

She heard a tap on glass and her gaze shot to the multi-paned window that looked out onto the porch and backyard. He was on the screened porch. She let out a breath, then, grabbing a cup of coffee and tucking the chart under her arm, she stepped out onto the porch. He was on the wicker sofa, his bare feet propped on the matching coffee table, a mug in his fist.

He looked up and she noticed the dark circles under his eyes.

"How long have you been out here?"

"A couple hours."

"You couldn't sleep? Are you in pain?" She touched his forehead, then set the cup down to take his pulse.

He pulled away. "I'm fine. Stop hovering and sit."

Her brows rose. *Unusually grouchy this morning,* she thought, and stepped over his legs to sit.

The sun was just rising, the land coated in a purple-orange haze. It felt familiar, the silence, the glowing sky—Rick beside her on the wicker sofa. If he didn't have to leave at the crack of dawn for some training operation, they'd shared that first cup of coffee right here. Although his time at home was rare, they'd made it a ritual.

She put her feet up, wiggling into the cushions.

"It's been awhile since I had a relaxing morning like this."

Rick glanced to the side. She had her head tipped back, her eyes closed. He wanted to kiss her senseless. "How so?"

"I'm working for two doctors. One's a surgeon. I'm constantly running between the offices and hospital to check on patients, and most times end up with the night shift."

That didn't sound fair to Rick, but then maybe she didn't have anyone to go home to, either. *Don't open that can of worms,* he warned himself, and kept his mouth shut.

"Civilians?"

"Yeah, and they like giving orders just as much as the military. But they're great people." A smile curved her lips and he wondered if she was thinking about some man. One he'd like to pound into the dirt right now.

A fresh headache brewing, he went to rub his forehead before he remembered he was laced into the sling like it was a straight jacket.

"I need to look at the stitches today and change the dressing."

"Later."

She lifted her head to look at him, rebellion in her green eyes. "I have a job to do, Rick." She reached for his coffee cup, eyeing him when he held on to it.

His eyes went dark and dangerous. "You're coming between a Marine and his cup of joe."

"Better call in reinforcements, then." She wrestled the nearly empty cup from him, set it aside, then reached across him and grasped his wrist. She took his pulse.

"God, what a nag," he teased.

She flashed him a smile, her hair falling over her shoulder. "I'm Irish. It's an art form." She let him go, gave him back his coffee, then opened a folder and jotted some notes.

Rick tipped his head to read. His name, rank and serial number were on the edge. "What are you doing with my records?"

"It's just a copy of your surgery report and instructions from Dr. Fisher."

Rick gave her a sidelong glance. "Studying up?"

"It helps to know exactly what they did." She closed the file, clipping the pen to the top. "And Dr. Fisher will want a report." Fisher was a Navy Captain, the equivalent to a Marine Colonel. "Full bird," as they called them.

"Heck, I don't even know what they did. It was a haze."

"Do you want to know?" She offered him the chart.

"Nah, as long as it'll heal, I don't care if they used staples and glue."

"Not quite, but close." Three different teams of doctors had kept him alive, but Dr. Fisher had taken over once Rick was stateside. He'd been sent back to the U.S. for the simple reason that there were so many wounded, they needed the space in Germany. Kate still didn't know the details of how he'd been wounded, and she told herself she probably didn't need to know.

Tossing the folder on the table, she stared at her cup, toying with the handle. "If you want to talk about it, I—"

"No," he interrupted. He wasn't about to tell her that one hellacious Technicolor nightmare had shown him every second of the attack last night. She'd want details. It was too ugly to share.

"I didn't think so."

He opened his mouth to say something, though he didn't know what, but she cut him off. "How about a fresh cup of coffee?"

Rick drained the dregs of his coffee as she stood and tried to maneuver around the table, then decided to step over his legs instead, just as he slid his feet off the table. She lost her balance, and with his good arm, he caught her around the waist and pulled. She landed on his lap.

"Whoa. You almost kissed the concrete."

"Yeah, thanks. Keep those gunboat feet out of the way, huh?" She wanted off, now. A second more and she'd be all over him.

She shifted to push off, and Rick groaned a curse.

She looked at him. "Did I hit your shoulder? Your hand?" A muscle in his jaw worked and Kate frowned, touching his face. "My stars, Rick, you're hot."

"You got that right."

His hand splayed over her hip, the warmth spiraling through her with the feel of his arousal against her hip. The fact that he was hard for her, right now, made her body hum.

"Rick. Let me up, you're going to hurt yourself."

His eyes darkened and he bent his legs, toppling her against him. "Not any more than I already am." His hand moved up her bare thigh.

Desire tumbled through her and she wanted his kiss, his touch. Right now, all over her. Yet she covered his hand, a warning in her eyes. "This won't solve anything, you know."

"It'll help a couple things." His fingers slid under the edge of her shorts, against naked skin. Kate was frozen, hunger battling with common sense. Then his hand moved, his fingertips sliding over her center, pressing, sending hot liquid shots of desire through her body. *More,* her mind begged. *More.* Then her brain kicked in.

"A temporary fix," she managed. With Herculean will, she gripped the arm of the sofa and pulled herself up, then looked back at him, noticing the bulge in his sweatpants and the look in his eye.

Hard and intense. She wondered if he was angry with her or himself. "Try to think of me as a...corpsman."

His gaze roamed her body in its shorts and T-shirt, her nipples outlined through the fabric. Knowing she was aroused made his own body flex with need. "That'd be easier if I didn't know what you look like naked."

His fierce gaze slid over her like warm wine, intoxicating her. Before this got dangerous, she picked up his cup and headed into the kitchen.

Rick stayed where he was, needing time to get a handle on his hunger, deciding he was behaving like a hormone challenged teenager around her. When he could stand, he went into the house, hunting in the cabinets for a toaster pastry. It tasted like ten-year-old MREs, and he reached for his coffee to wash it down.

Kate was rooting in the fridge, her behind displayed for him.

"Trust me, Kate, the grocery fairy didn't show up during the night."

Suddenly she popped up, as if she'd suddenly thought of something. "How about pancakes?" She stepped to the cabinet and pulled out an unopened box of pancake mix. "I forgot I saw this in here yesterday. No doubt it's been here awhile, but it's unopened so it should be okay."

He nodded, watching as she moved around the kitchen, dragging out bowls, a skillet and syrup.

He missed seeing her in here, moving like a professional—efficient, quick. Sexy as hell. She'd fallen in love with the wide-open kitchen with the view to the backyard the instant the Realtor had shown it to them. Rick glanced around. Everything was exactly as she'd left it, minus a couple of burned potholders.

"Sit down, Rick. Before you pass out."

He gave her a sour look, but sat on a stool at the end of the island. He simply watched her, remembering her cooking Thanksgiving dinner for her family the first time. She'd been a nervous wreck, making way too much food. But it had been picture perfect. He'd been so proud of her.

He missed her family, too, he thought. Loud, Irish and happy to argue good-naturedly at the drop of a hat, they'd welcomed him into their fold so easily it had shocked him. Before Kate, he'd been on the outside, and now he was there again.

"How're your brothers?"

Finished preparing the batter, she ladled spoonfuls on the hot griddle. "They're fine. Mom and Dad are on a cruise. Their third." She shrugged. "The Yucatan this time, I think. Connor's working on the West Coast, enjoying being single. We've resigned ourselves that he will never marry." She flipped the pancakes.

It was on the tip of Rick's tongue to say her brother hadn't found the right woman, but he kept his mouth shut. Rick had found the right one and look where they were.

"Sean and Laura are in Texas. His construction company's doing well enough. And Michael…"

She stopped, staring down at the pancakes, then quickly put them on a plate before him.

"Kate? What's wrong? What's up with Mike?"

She lifted his gaze to Rick's as she handed him silverware and syrup. "Nothing. He and Carol are fine."

Rick frowned, cutting into the pancakes. "That's not all, is it?"

"No." She took a deep breath and ladled more batter onto the griddle. "It's good news, actually." Her voice had gone unusually bright. "Michael's going to be a father for the first time."

Rick's features tightened, the words hitting him like a frontal assault. Kate had wanted children. Rick hadn't. He'd felt that the two of them were enough, and admitted that he didn't think he was father material. He hadn't had a role model to know what being a parent was, not to mention a good one, but that wasn't the main problem.

Little kids scared the hell out of him. Give him a hundred raw fresh-out-of-boot-camp Marines and he was fine. But turn a baby loose anywhere near him and he was useless. He couldn't keep his wife; what made him think he could ever be a dad?

His career was too risky for kids, he reasoned, just

as another voice screamed that most Marines had families and did just fine. He jabbed at the pancakes, eating without tasting. But Kate had accepted his feelings on the subject before, and if she didn't understand them, the fact that she wasn't living here and his recent, almost deadly injuries were speaking loud enough now.

Kids would have been a huge mistake. Especially caught in this mess. "That's great for them," he said, focusing on his meal.

"Carol will deliver around April."

Rick looked up, noticing a strange look in Kate's eyes. Slowly, he set the fork down. "They'll make great parents."

"Yes, they will. Michael said he was scared and excited. He's never even held a baby before."

Neither had Rick. "Tell them congratulations for me, will you?"

She nodded, her gaze on the pancakes sizzling on the griddle. He stood, brought his plate to the sink and thanked her for the meal. She murmured something unintelligible, her back to him as she scooped up the remaining pancakes. She slid the pan off the burner and faced him.

When Rick expected a confrontation, he got cool and dictatorial.

"You need to take your medication." She stepped around him, doling it out.

Rick took the painkiller, wanting the foggy oblivion right now. Anything was better than seeing the heartache in her eyes. He headed out of the kitchen.

He was heading for cover, Kate thought, watching him go. Whether Rick admitted it or not, she knew the real reason he didn't want to discuss kids. He didn't want a permanent tie to anyone. Because to have a baby with her would be creating a solid, unbreakable bond even he couldn't ignore.

For a man who'd grown up alone all his life, she'd have thought he would jump at the chance of being a father, making a family, putting down roots. But not Rick. She'd come from a large family and wanted one of her own, but his attitude sent that dream up in smoke.

It was probably good he didn't know that a couple weeks after leaving him, she'd learned she was pregnant. She'd tried to reach him, but he'd been on a mission, out of contact. Telling him now would be pointless. And painful. He didn't want her enough to come after her, but a baby would have made him feel obligated. She didn't want him that way, as if it was a duty.

But then, she didn't have their baby anymore, did she?

And she didn't have him, either.

Four

Rick knew when it was wise to retreat and duck for cover. So when she started barking orders like a drill instructor, he complied, lying on his bed so she could change the dressings. She'd been quiet for the last hour and it made him wary. A quiet Kate O'Malley Wyatt was not a good thing.

It meant that an explosion was coming. Which usually involved a short quick argument ending with some wild sex. It's what he loved about her. When she wanted to kiss and make up, she left nothing to chance. But now she wore that determined look of a trained nurse ready to do battle.

With a stack of sterile supply trays wrapped in plastic, she sat beside him, removed the sling, his shirt, then peeled back the bandages above the cast. Her touch was delicate and careful, but he couldn't look at her.

"How many have you got of those?" He nodded to the sterile packs.

"The Navy hospital gave me several. They were generous. But then, you hold a special place in Lieutenant Roker's heart."

Rick made a face. "She's a warhorse who doesn't know the words *let me sleep*. That woman poked and prodded at the strangest hours." It was the reason he'd asked to leave the hospital. That and sheer boredom.

"You loved it. She was quite taken, mentioned something about a sponge bath."

His gaze zeroed in on Kate like a heat-seeking missile. "I like the one I had with you more."

Something momentarily softened in her eyes, dived right into his heart and stirred him up. Then she was all-business.

"Be still. When you get the stationary pins out it will be easier to move around without them bumping into things."

As she spoke, she opened the pack, arranging mountains of gauze, then unrolled what looked like surgical instruments. "You know how to use all that?" he asked.

"Of course. We use them in E.R., most times we have to do triage surgery. But I've trained as a surgical nurse for the past year." She'd had to do something to use up the time alone or she'd have gone crazy. Watching the door, listening for the phone that never rang.

She placed his cast on a pillow. "You have to keep the shoulder immobile so the internal stitches can heal. Moving it around will tear them, and you could end up back in surgery. So promise me you won't try to use this arm."

When he didn't say anything, she looked at him.

His brows shot up. "You want actual words?"

"Yes."

"Don't trust me?"

"When it comes to you not pushing yourself to heal faster than you can? Nope, not a lick."

"I promise."

She made a comical noise like a crowd cheering. "Victory! Ohh-rah." She grinned, then said, "Now just relax and this will go a lot easier."

"They always say that when it's going to hurt."

"Is that fear I hear?"

"Do your worst, Miss Nightingale."

Carefully, she peeled back the layers of padding, and when she saw his wound, she swallowed and forced her features to remain still. "Looks like someone already did." He'd been shot in the back, and while there was a clean hole there, the exit wound was tattered.

Rick watched her, and while he admired her

methodically efficient nursing skills, it felt cold to him. As if his Kate had stepped out and someone else was within his grasp as she leaned over him, cleaning the wound, inspecting the stitches.

"It's looking good. Can you lift your arm a little?" He did, but when it started to tremble violently, she laid it back down on the pillow.

He cursed.

"It will get better, Rick," she told him. "The wound nicked an artery. You're lucky you didn't bleed to death."

He knew that, and thanked God for the Navy corpsman attached to his unit who'd rushed through gunfire to help him.

Kate sterilized the area, not at all shocked when he didn't flinch, didn't move. After redressing the wound, she helped him back into the sling. She knew he was in pain, his breathing hard, yet his expression didn't change. She collected her instruments and left to put them in a basin, and when she returned, he was out cold. She checked his pulse, satisfied the painkillers had kicked in.

She left him to sleep, but stopped in the hall, grabbing the wall and covering her mouth, muffling the sobs trying to escape. Her heart broke for him. Rick was a Marine down to his bones, in his soul, and from the looks of that wound, he might never be one again.

It would destroy him.

* * *

Rick woke to the sound of voices. Women's voices. Lots of them. He managed to dress in jeans and a T-shirt, but skipped the shoes and socks. He moved down the hall cautiously, waiting for the attack of females he could hear laughing and chatting away in the kitchen. Some voices sounded familiar, and when he stepped inside, he wasn't as stunned as he might be.

Marine wives had infiltrated his kitchen. They'd regrouped and brought supplies. The island counter was laden with covered dishes and cakes, plastic containers of food. There was even a couple bottles of wine and a stack of books. Kate stood near the end of the counter, smiling, pouring coffee, slicing a breakfast cake someone had obviously brought. She looked so happy right now the sight struck him in the chest.

His gaze moved over the group of about a dozen women, recognizing his commanding officer's wife, and the Sergeant Major's wife, right beside her as always. The room quieted as one by one they noticed him. They all stared, and he felt suddenly self-conscious of his bare feet.

"Good morning, ladies."

They murmured a greeting, looking back and forth from him to Kate. He felt as if he were standing inspection, they were staring so hard.

Kate heard a couple envious sighs from the women. Rick's snug black T-shirt and worn jeans were enough to give her palpitations. Add to that the sexy, sleepy-eyed look and he made her want to drag him into the bedroom and have her way with him. Rick caught her gaze and, as if he recognized the look, he winked.

The Colonel's wife, Janet, stood, coming around the table edge. "How are you feeling, Captain?" She moved toward him, deep concern in her eyes.

"Better than I was a few days ago, ma'am."

"Alan called me just afterward." Her gaze flicked to the cast and bandages. "You look better than I expected."

"Thank you, ma'am."

"Look, Rick. Food." Kate glanced at her friends. "Apparently they're aware of your culinary skills and sent in rations."

"Honey, we did it for you," Kelly, the Sergeant Major's wife, said. "We're all so glad you survived, Captain."

There was a collective nodding of agreement.

"It could have easily been one of our husbands."

"I appreciate this, ma'am, ladies." He nodded to the others, still feeling on display. It was tough being the only one of the battalion back home, even if he was wounded.

"Well, you have the best of care with Kate. In that we won't worry."

"When we didn't see Kate at the predeployment formation, we wondered why," a young wife said. A couple other women nudged her.

Kate blushed and started to speak, not knowing what she'd say that wouldn't embarrass them both, but Rick spoke up.

"We said our goodbyes in private the night before." With a devilish grin, he slipped up beside her and put his arm around her shoulder. "And Kate had an emergency at the hospital that morning. I figured saving a life was more important than seeing me off with a thousand smelly grunts."

They laughed, but Kate stared up at him, realizing he'd saved her many uncomfortable questions about their relationship—maybe even her reputation—with that bald-faced lie. He kissed the top of her head, and when she looked up at him, she wondered just how much of Rick she wasn't seeing because she wanted to *hear* him express his feelings.

What if she was the one who'd failed them? She'd hoped that by her leaving and spending some time apart, he would have been moved to action. But what if he was just as scared as she was? She felt suddenly ashamed of herself. As if sensing it, Rick stayed beside her, leaning on her, touching her and joining in the conversation. When the Colonel's wife stood to say goodbye, like a well-trained squad, the women all headed for the door. Kate saw them out, hugging each one.

After they'd left she closed the door and looked at him, grinning. "Want to pig out? Janet, Kelly and Christine are the best cooks in the battalion."

Like kids cut loose from the shadow of a parent, they went into the kitchen, investigating the dishes and sampling everything.

"You're a better cook."

"I won't tell the Colonel's wife you said that." Kate glanced up, her smile mischievous. "But thanks, I haven't cooked in a while."

"No fun doing it for one, huh?"

She went still for a second. "No, Rick, it's not."

He heard the bite in her tone, and sighed. "Kate, how about we call a truce?"

"I wasn't aware we were at war."

"If we keep butting heads we will be, and I don't want that."

"Yes, you need to rest."

"It's not that," he snapped, then took a breath. More softly he said, "I just don't want to walk around on eggshells—and you shouldn't have to, not when you're helping me."

She met his gaze over a pot roast that was still steaming. "Agreeing to disagree?"

"Yeah."

"Deal."

He dug a fork into the center of a cherry pie, and she shrieked. "Rick, stop that!" She cut a generous slice and served it on a plate. "Your manners have gone to the dogs. Next you'll be drinking right out of the milk carton."

"Possible. No one around to keep me in line." He winked again and her heart dipped.

"Go to the couch." She pointed the way.

"Ma'am, yes ma'am."

Rick smiled on his way back into the living room, thinking it had taken so little to get a rise out of her again. His mind latched on to the other ways he could do that, and he sat, groaning, and eating cherry pie without really tasting it.

This is your mess, he thought, and not for the first time. *How are you going to fix it?*

It was after midnight when Kate heard a strange noise—a deep groan laced with agony. She left her bed and hurried into the master bedroom. In the dark, Rick twisted and writhed, a nightmare locking him in its grip. She came to the bedside, calling his name, afraid that his thrashing would break the stitches or bump a pin. She leaned closer.

"Rick, honey, it's over. You're here with me."

Yet the dream raged on. He twisted on the sheets, muttering something that sounded like commands. *He's reliving the battle in his dreams.* He was breathing hard, his face contorted, his fist clenched. She pressed a knee to the mattress and started to wake him, then remembered that when she'd startled him awake in the past, he would come up swinging, fist primed. He could injure himself further, she thought, and bent low, whispering his name.

It hurt to see him so tortured, straining against invisible bonds, damning the gunfire going on around him in his dreams. She leaned close to his ear.

"Rick, it's a dream. Wake up."

"My men," he muttered.

"They're out of danger. Reinforcements are here," she said, hoping he'd calm down. He was going to rip the stitches open. He arched sharply, flailing, and Kate shifted closer, laying her hand on his brow. He was sweating, but clammy and cold, and her eyes teared up. What had he suffered?

"It's over," she said softly.

"Kate," he moaned, his eyes still closed.

"I'm here, darling. I'm here." She curled in beside him, reassuring him. He calmed, his breathing softening, and she kissed his cheek, pressing a hand over his wildly beating heart. "I'm here, Rick."

"Don't leave me." His voice broke.

And her heart shattered, her eyes burning. Suddenly, she needed to hold him, and settled closer. She laid her head on his uninjured shoulder, stroking his face, his arm, waiting until he drifted into a peaceful sleep.

A serene contentment enveloped her, warm and safe and needed. It was deceiving, and she fought the urge to stay right there and sink into her own dreams. Certain he was sleeping peacefully, she slipped off the bed and padded back to the guest room.

She wanted to stay, but Rick wouldn't want her to know she'd seen him like that. It brought new questions. Was she hoping for a change in him that wasn't going to happen? He was a private person, but she felt it was from years of being so alone and isolated, tossed through the foster care system, then dumped on an uncle who couldn't have cared less about him.

Maybe Rick had expected her to leave, too, and had kept himself back in case she did?

And then, damn her heart, she'd gone and done so, confirming his worst fears by walking out.

Rick was groggy when he woke the next morning. That was the reason he hated talking pills. It felt like a cloud fuzzed his brain, making his reactions slow, his thoughts jumbled. Nightmares did that worse than the drugs, yet last night's dream hadn't been as bad as the others. Vaguely, he remembered dreaming of Kate's touch, hearing her voice drift through his mind. He could almost feel her body pressed to his side. He shook his head, deciding that he was fabricating it all because she was here, so close and so untouchable.

He walked into the kitchen and poured a cup of coffee. When he heard music, he followed the sound to the back porch. He stopped in the doorway, smiling.

Now that was a pleasant sight—Kate bent over the lawnmower, adding gas. But his attention zipped right to her shorts, frayed cutoffs hinting at the curves of her behind. The skin-tight pink tank top hugged her breasts, proving she wasn't wearing anything under it.

Going to be a helluva morning, he thought, already feeling the strain to his body.

Not making himself known, he sat on the wicker sofa and propped his feet on the table, his arm on a pillow. No reason to piss her off when she was giving him such a nice view. He wanted to help, but knew she'd force him into submission.

As she had last night. They'd sat around like pals, watching movies, not getting too near, not touching the topic of their impending divorce. It made Rick sick to think about it, but he was treading carefully, and wisely, kept his mouth shut and just enjoyed being with her again. He'd missed her so damn much, and for a while there it felt like it used to be—a little exciting to be near her, and comfortable knowing she was around.

He nursed his coffee, watching as she pulled the rip cord and started the engine. She wore a pair of women's combat boots he'd bought for her, and a red USMC baseball cap. She mowed the back lawn around the small swimming pool while Rick admired the muscles in her thighs and her tight behind in the sexy shorts. He'd been so proud to have her as his wife—not because she was drop-dead gorgeous as much as the fact that she had a heart as big as the country. Being here, despite their troubles, proved it again.

The engine stopped and she moved the mower to one side. When she saw him, she stopped in her tracks.

"How long have you been up?"

He told her. "You've been at it early." He gestured to the couple dozen nursery pots of flowers ready to be planted.

She shielded her eyes as she walked closer. "Already out to the grocery store and back. I thought these would look nice. You don't mind, do you?"

"Of course not, and stop asking me about stuff like it's not your home, too." She opened her mouth, and he shot to his feet. "I know what I said, but it is."

"Does that mean I get to take over the bathroom?"

He groaned. "God, no."

Smiling, she dusted off her hands as she entered the screened porch. "How are you feeling?"

"Outstanding."

She eyed him, then frowned. "Sit down."

"I'm tired of sitting. I'm tired of doing nothing."

"Too bad. Play a video game."

"With one hand?"

"Duck hunt?"

He smirked. "Not a challenge."

"Janet left books. Read one."

"Maybe later."

"What can I help you with?" she asked.

"Nothing," he fairly snarled.

Kate let that glide off her, knowing he'd had a nightmare last night. "Then come out and sit while I plant."

She grabbed a lawn chair and a pillow and he followed her out into the sun. Rick took the pillow, his gaze warning her away, and she knelt and started digging.

"Seeing anyone?" he asked.

She jerked around to stare at him. How could he ask that? she thought in annoyance then she took a breath. "No, you?"

"Obviously not, if you're here and she's not."

"You're a lousy patient. I'm not surprised."

"There isn't anyone else, Kate. There never will be."

She froze and met his gaze. He hadn't said anything like that to her in a long long time. What was she supposed to say? Thanks? Good to know? *If there won't be anyone else, then why can't you confide in me?* He was her husband. In some ways they'd shared as much as two people could, and knew each other intimately. Rick's "keep it all in" was what had ruined the core of their marriage.

She didn't say anything, but stood, leaning down to kiss him tenderly. She couldn't form words, couldn't express what that meant to her in any other way.

Then she went back to planting.

But Kate was having more than second thoughts. Heck, they'd plagued her for days after she'd left, when she'd learned she was pregnant with a child he'd never wanted. She'd lain in a hospital knowing she was losing the only connection to him, and that he hadn't wanted any bonds that tight.

And if the last few days were any indication, those bonds were still unwanted.

Five

Rick didn't know what was ticking him off—her reaction to what he'd told her, or his inability to understand his own wife after all this time. He'd expected more from her, and for a woman who wanted him to express himself, she wasn't upping the ante any. He'd spent far too much time dissecting that kiss, and by dinner, he was sawing one handed into his sirloin steak as if he was cutting barbed wire.

He was being stubborn by refusing her help—that much he recognized—but as if fate interfered, his weak grip slipped.

The knife clattered to the floor just as his fork went airborne like a grenade, arching high.

"Incoming," Kate said, and they both watched it land on the kitchen floor. She looked at him, her lips twitching.

"Go on," he groused sourly. "Let it out. You look like you're going to bust a gut."

She lost it, her laughter filling the house like music. He'd missed that sound.

"I'd say my point was made rather well," she teased.

He pushed the plate toward her. "Fine, go ahead."

She retrieved the flying fork, set it in the sink and then pulled her chair close to cut his steak for him.

"Want a bib, too?"

"Want me to stuff a rag in your mouth?"

"Like that would do any good." She grinned, speared a piece of meat and held it poised at his mouth.

"I can manage from here." He snapped up the bite anyway, then took the fresh fork from her.

"I saw new woodworking stuff in the garage."

"It's just some basic tools, and a project I'd started."

"I didn't know you liked building things."

"I didn't, either. It was sheer boredom and watching way too many home and garden shows that did it."

"Garden?"

"I was making a window box." He thought for a second. "I think that's what it was. I didn't get very far before the last deployment. The Sergeant Major was teaching me. He's a real whiz at it."

"I've seen some of his recent work."

"Yeah? When?"

"When I was at Kelly's for a coffee with the wives."

"You haven't been for a year."

She arched a brow. "Says who?"

He frowned.

"I still keep in touch. I didn't want them to know, either. It's not like they wouldn't speculate when we weren't seen together."

"At least my men keep a lid on talk."

She laughed shortly. "Ha, who are you fooling? They're the worst. Oh, they'll never reveal classified stuff, but if you think men don't gossip, you're wrong. Everyone has an opinion, and everyone is looking for something to pick at to avoid looking at their own lives."

Rick winced, thinking how he'd immersed himself in work rather than come home to an empty house. Avoiding the issues, he thought sourly. "Well then, my men are still over there, *gossiping* and not cleaning their weapons."

She liked his teasing smile. That was the Rick she remembered. "They've only got a couple weeks till they return. And I'm betting they're anxious to know how you are, though I'm sure Janet reported to her husband, and Kelly to the Sergeant Major. You'll be the talk of the camp."

"What a thrill."

There was a stretch of silence before she said, "Were you afraid?"

He looked up. "No."

She made a face, clearly not buying that.

"I wasn't." He shrugged. "Not till I got hit. I was afraid I'd lose consciousness and someone else would die because I wasn't watching their six." *And that I'd never see you again,* he added silently. She'd been his only thought the instant he'd realized he was shot. He'd had to force her out of his mind, tend to his wound until the corpsman reached him. But she'd never left his thoughts, and he'd prayed he'd live long enough to have another chance to hold her.

Hadn't he sworn to himself that he'd take that chance when he was well enough to get to her? That he wouldn't let her slip away again? As if he'd *let* her slip away. She'd been right before. He hadn't stopped her; he had just accepted. Why, when he wouldn't accept defeat on the battlefield, did he give up so easily with the only person he loved more than living?

War and love were not fair.

"You're such a hero," she teased, batting her lashes and fanning herself.

"Yeah, but I can't cut my own steak."

"That's why you have me," she said primly.

"I can think of other reasons to have you."

She looked up, and his gaze locked on her like a target. Kate could almost feel it touch her skin, and every inch of her body sprang to life with a desire so strong it demanded satisfaction. *Right now.* Her skin tingled; the area between her thighs flushed. Before their separation, Rick and she would have been tearing at each other on the floor by now. But that was then.

"Or rather, *ways* to have you."

"Rick…"

"I won't hide the fact that you light me up like a nuclear warhead, Kate."

"So you like walking around all…" She gestured to his jeans.

"Hard for you?" He grinned at her sweet blush. "Better than being dead."

Her teasing smile melted instantly. "Don't say that!" She stared at him, her lower lip trembling, memories of seeing him torn and bleeding ripping through her mind. "Don't ever say that!"

She started to leave the table, but he covered her hand with his and kept her there. "I'm okay, baby."

"But you could have *died*."

"We both knew that could happen."

"Yes, I knew that! But I don't want a folded flag, Rick. I don't want the regrets of a grateful nation. Don't do this again."

"I can't promise that and you know it."

She let out a breath. She should be used to this, and wondered if the Sergeant Major's wife ever was. Or Janet. Their husbands had been in the Marines for over twenty-five years. Kate didn't bother to remind herself that she and Rick were legally separated. Her feelings were strong and wounded, and still focused on him.

She didn't want to be free of him, and as she lifted her gaze, she knew she *had* to use this chance for something more than helping him get back to the career he loved enough to take a bullet.

"I know," she muttered as she stood to gather plates.

He caught her around the waist, pulling her close.

"I'll watch my six, I swear. If for no other reason than not to see that look in your eyes."

Her throat tightened and she leaned down and whispered, "Right now, *I'm* watching that six. And it's such a nice backside to see." Then she kissed him.

Rick didn't let it stay chaste; pulling her down on his lap and devouring her mouth. He was starved for her, his hand sliding up her bare thigh to her breast. He cupped her, massaged her and her soft moan was a gift. His hand roamed, his tongue dipped and teased. He could feel the heat building in her.

"God, I've missed you."

"Sex or me?"

"I'm a guy. I can't separate the two."

She smiled against his mouth, still balancing the plates and kissed him some more. Then she stood, and as if nothing had happened, she went to the sink.

"Forget those, I'll help with them later."

"They're my grandmother's dishes, Rick. Did I ever let you handle them?"

"There is a first time for everything."

"Yeah, sure. When you have two working hands, maybe."

That hit him hard, again. "God, I hate being helpless."

She sighed, dropping her head forward. "You know what?" She faced him. "I'm sick of this bitching."

"Excuse me?"

"So you can't do for yourself and you don't like it. Big deal. Get over it, Marine. In the grand scheme of things that *could have* happened to you, not being able to cut meat or shower without falling is pretty minor."

He blinked up at her. It was the explosion he'd been waiting for.

"Is that who you are, Rick? Two hands? I sure as heck don't see you that way. You're a Marine. Improvise, adapt, overcome."

"With you jumping down my throat when I try to do anything?"

"Because you're fighting your own recovery!"

She moved in like a wild tigress—in his face—and he fought his smile. She looked magnificent, her eyes flashing brightly, her cheeks flushed.

"You were shot, for pity's sake. You can't expect to magically be in peak Marine condition because it annoys you. Part of improvising is asking for help. Part of overcoming pain is doing the things you need to so you're *not* hurting. You have three more days of complete rest, and when the stitches come out—if you be-have—I'll ask the doctors to cut down the pins so they won't be in the way so much. Once they're removed, it's smooth sailing till you start with therapy. So—" she cocked her hip, folded her arms "—how about you make this a little easier on both of us and stop re-fusing my orders, and just do them!"

"Anything else, ma'am?" he said, his lips stretch-ing in a wide grin.

It startled her. "Yeah. Behave. Don't try to lift any-thing, do anything, with that arm, so I can take a bath without worrying."

"I will park my six on the sofa." He crossed his heart.

She eyed him doubtfully.

"Unless you're going to let me watch."

Her cheeks reddened.

He leaned down in her face, his husky voice driv-ing through her like a blade. "It's not like I haven't seen and kissed *and* tasted every inch of you."

Kate sputtered, then simply pointed to the living room, but her hand trembled. Heck, her whole body trembled.

Rick arched a brow with a sexy look, giving her an-other chance to reconsider.

Kate knew she was about to give in so she straight-ened her shoulders and pointed harder. "Go, now. Sofa. On the double. Or *I'll* take those stitches out with a butter knife!"

He spun around and marched out, smiling to himself over that little outburst. Even if she tried to smother her feelings now and then, he'd seen them in her eyes, and it gave Rick a sense of purpose he'd lost when she'd walked away.

Kate came out of the bathroom feeling relaxed and ready for a glass of wine. She poured one, taking it with her to the living room. Rick was sifting through movie DVDs when she sat on the sofa.

He glanced up, his gaze traveling swiftly over her Doris Day pajamas, the satin thin and clinging to her curves.

"Is that chick camouflage?" he said.

She glanced down. "Comfort."

"I remember a little red number you had." He wiggled his brows.

"Little is right."

"It looked good tossed on the bedroom floor."

Inside she went absolutely giddy with desire, then smothered it, leaning over to look at the movies. She plucked one out, waiting for some grief from him. But he took it and loaded it in the player.

"You'll like it."

"I doubt it. Nothing explodes in this movie."

She nudged him. "Give it a chance." Kate busied herself with propping pillows for him and fussing during the credits.

He caught her hand. "Are you going to hover all the time?"

"I'm a nurse. It's what I do best."

"No more nurse tonight, okay?"

She sat down on the sofa, then propped her feet on the coffee table.

A half hour later, Rick was still watching. Kate was sound asleep beside him. Smiling to himself when she wiggled into the cushions, he scooted closer and she snuggled to his side, her hand on his stomach. He wouldn't wake her. She'd been doing so much since she showed up, besides driving him nuts.

After the movie, which was good even if nothing blew up, he turned off the set and shifted so she was more comfortable. His uninjured arm around her, Rick closed his eyes, thankful that she was in his arms, even if she didn't know it or want it.

Early in the morning, Rick was dangling his feet in the pool, reading the latest thriller and trying not to drop the book in the water, when a sudden blast of noise from the house made him glance up.

What the hell?

He was up and moving fast, the book discarded. He burst in the back of the house and winced at the music combined with the vacuum. He didn't know which was worse or louder, but when he walked into the living room, Kate was dancing to some old Temptations music as if the vacuum were her partner. She looked like she was having a blast.

She'd always cleaned or cooked to music, just not quite this loud.

He leaned against the nearest wall, watching her hips gyrate, her breasts bounce quite nicely. And when she did that hip curling motion that was too much like she did when they were making love and she was on top, Rick decided he was just asking for punishment.

He called to her.

She paused and looked around, smiling when she found him. She shut off the vac.

"Is that necessary?" He gesture to the stereo.

"Just putting a little do in my honey-do list. Breakfast is on the table for you."

He smiled as she turned back to the world's most boring chore, then went into the kitchen. He sat down to the enormous meal she'd prepared, catching a glimpse of her through the doorway as she bebopped down the hall. Amused, he shook his head.

He felt better this morning, less groggy. No nightmares. Kate had slept beside him on the couch until three in the morning, and when he woke, he was covered with a blanket, his legs on the sofa, and she was gone. Dammit. How was he supposed to win her back if she kept her distance?

A few minutes later all was quiet and she started to join him, then noticed a lightbulb was out in the kitchen.

"I can do that," he offered.

"Orders…" she reminded him, and grabbed the step stool and bulb, climbing up. She wasn't tall and had to stretch. Rick rose out of his chair just as she lost her balance. She shrieked and he caught her with his good arm. Her feet dangled off the floor.

"Rick! Put me down. You'll hurt yourself."

He met her gaze head-on. "I'll never let you fall," he said, setting her down.

Her breath caught at the strength of his tone. She stared at him for a long moment, then said, "Let me check your stitches."

He snatched her wrists. "I'm fine, no pain. I swear."

"Okay, okay." She climbed onto the step stool again, and this time Rick held her steady. The bare skin of her thighs was cool beneath his hands and he wanted to stroke her a little higher, under those shorts, but she'd probably fall again.

"How about a swim after breakfast?"

She eyed him and stepped down.

"Okay, I'll sit, you swim."

Good grief, he was really bored, Kate thought. While the house had come with a pool, Rick rarely used it because it wasn't long enough for laps. Floating around lazily wasn't his idea of fun.

"Sure. I'll get the sleeve." She smirked up at him. "Think you could manage getting those jeans off, or do you need he—"

He eyed her.

"I'll let you slide this time."

He went to change and when he returned, she was already out by the pool, a couple of lounge chairs set up, with towels. Rick stopped short when he saw her in her bathing suit—if that's what you'd call it. She couldn't put on a one-piece? Did she have to wear that skimpy thing? Then he remembered she'd bought it for him, swearing she wouldn't be seen in public in something so sparse.

It barely covered her.

And she must have seen something in his expression because she adjusted it and said, "I found it in an old beach bag. I didn't bring a suit."

Like that mattered?

The bright pink flowered bikini was nothing more than a couple of triangles. Rick groaned as he sat in a lounge chair, wondering how long it would take for him to go clinically insane with hunger for his own wife. He lay back, closed his eyes and absorbed the sun. When he heard the splash of water, he cracked open one eye. Okay—wet, she was worse. Well...better, actually.

Diving off the board wasn't much help, either. Everything bounced. If he wasn't half covered in plaster and stitched up, he'd try his damndest to get her into bed.

She swam to him, leaning on the edge of the pool.

"You can get in with the sleeve, you know. I can blow up an inner tube or the float."

"Maybe later. The flowers look nice." He nodded to the flower beds she had planted the day before.

She glanced around, admiring them. "Till I kill them."

"Your green thumb is a little tainted."

She made a sour face, but didn't deny the truth.

"You have other talents. Want to test them out?"

Her attention snapped back to him. "Are you trying to provoke me?"

"I guess that depends to what end."

"I'm not sleeping with you. That won't help things between us."

"You're avoiding the question."

"I refuse to answer on the grounds that it might ruin this lovely day."

He shook his head. "Not good enough, babe. Truth."

"Oh, we're doing truth or dare?"

Oops, he thought. "One truth."

"Yes, I still want you." Like mad, like crazy. It was taking everything she had to keep from provoking *him.*

Explosions went off inside him. "Now?"

"Don't go there. My turn. A truth."

He braced himself.

"What was the first thought that went through your mind when you realized you'd been hit?"

He leaned forward in the lounge chair, his gaze locked with hers. His voice was smooth and buttery soft when he said, "You, Kate."

She blinked.

"I wanted to stay alive to see you again."

Her eyes burned, and she saw the honesty in his expression. Kate felt as if she'd just been given a gift.

His gaze raked her as if he was seeing her for the first time. "God, I've missed you. *You*," he stressed. "Not sex. Well, there is that." He flashed a devilish smile. "But I've felt…"

She waited, breathless.

"…empty."

Kate glanced away, her throat tightening. It was a step, she thought, looking back at him when he spoke again.

"It was like being thrown back into the orphanage or foster homes. I didn't have a place anymore."

Her heart aching, she left the water, grabbing a towel and wrapping it around herself as she sat beside him. He lay back in the lounge chair, holding her hand. "When I was on that plane from Kandahar, I was so doped up, but I kept thinking, I'll never recover enough for Recon again. And I didn't have you, so then what?"

"You will be fit. I'm here to make sure of it."

"Why are you doing this, Kate? I know it's not easy for you. It sure isn't for me."

"Because no matter what's happened between us,

I know being a Marine is what you love. You won't stop being a perpetual grouch till you're back to full speed."

His thumb made a slow circle over the back of her hand. He leaned forward, bringing it to his lips for a kiss. "Thank you."

Kate's heart tore a little. She wanted to beg him to tell her more of his feelings, but she suspected they were locked up in some private spot that he didn't even share with himself. Part of her said, *Leave him be, it's just the way he is.* But pure Irish stubbornness told her that this was where they went wrong. She'd never felt totally his, never felt completely intimate with him because he wouldn't share his past. His pain. She suspected there was more to his reasons for not confiding in her, a little insecurity he'd never admit to having, maybe. Yet she savored this moment more than anything. It gave her something she hadn't thought she'd find again: hope.

A dark cloud moved into her thoughts, and she wondered what would happen when he learned she'd been pregnant with his child.

A day later Rick was wondering if she was deliberately torturing him. A week later he was an idiot.

She pranced around in the sexiest clothes, showing off more skin, and he was almost willing to give up national secrets if she'd stay closer, kiss him like she had before.

He stood in the shower, knowing she was outside the door. He could hear her humming. He was managing fine. She'd installed one of those soap dispensers for him, but insisted on being nearby in case he needed anything. He didn't mind, except his thoughts were locked on dragging her into the shower with him. Of course, he couldn't actually *do* anything worthwhile, and that put a damper on his desire. A little. Very little. But things would change. He was getting the stitches taken out this morning.

He felt like a kid going to see Santa.

Not that he'd ever done that when he was a child. Although Kate could take the stitches out herself, the surgeon had to give the okay. Kate had gone beyond the call and had given him a decent military haircut, but she'd convinced him that as much as he wanted to be back in uniform, it just wouldn't work around the cast, pins and bandages.

He shut off the water and stepped out. She was there with towels, and he let her be Nurse Nelly. He'd been doing anything to keep her by him, to provoke her care. And the way she was drying him off said he was getting to her.

As she was to him.

All day, every second. Man. He wanted her. So much that all he had to do was think about it and he was ready.

She wrapped the towel around his waist and then worked the plastic sleeve off.

"I've got to change. You going to be okay?"

"Sure, fine. But you look nice now," he said, taking in the miniskirt and sleeveless top she was wearing.

"Oh, I don't think so."

"Why?"

"This is not the attire of a Company Commander's wife."

"But we're separated. Legally."

She looked so hurt just then, he could have kicked himself.

"Not to anyone in the battalion. And it doesn't matter." She turned sharply and left.

She was dressing up for him, he thought, giving the public the best impression. It made him smile, even as he decided their relationship was like one of those spinning plates balancing on a stick. Keep the stick wiggling or they'd crash.

A half hour later, he was pacing by the front door when she came out, looking too damn sexy in a red blouse and skirt. His gaze lowered to her stocking-covered legs and the high-heeled pumps. He whistled softly and she blushed, smoothing the line of her skirt.

"You know…I don't have a weapon to fend off the troops. I'd hate to have to clean someone's clock today."

She rolled her eyes, smiling and nudging him out the door. "Me too, since that would be disobeying *my* orders—*command* orders—and you'd end up in the brig, ruin your reputation and wouldn't get that cherry lollipop after you get your stitches out."

He chuckled. "I think I'd risk it. Even for a cherry sucker."

Kate smiled and climbed behind the wheel. Yet Rick's mind locked on one fact.

With the stitches out and all the heavy bandages gone, he could do more. Not much, but whatever it was, he planned on doing it with her.

Six

In the kitchen, Kate had the radio going as Rick moved in behind her, swift and silent.

"What's up?"

She hopped out of the chair so fast it fell back. "For heaven's sake, Rick. Don't creep up on me like that!" she said, covering her heart.

"Sorry." The apology lost something when he gave her that sexy lopsided smirk that sent her pulse into overdrive. Then he examined the fabrics and machine on the kitchen table. He'd forgotten that she'd left it here. "Sewing? I haven't seen you sew in years."

"I know. If it's straight lines, I can manage."

"What's it going to be? Because I can't tell." He lifted the corner of some fabric and foam.

"It's a pad for your shoulder and neck," she explained, as if he should know. When his brows shot up, she added, "The sling strap is chafing." She reached out and touched his throat where it was already red this morning. "Since you have to wear it for a long time, I thought…" She shrugged, suddenly feeling silly.

"It's better than the towel I was going to stuff there. I didn't think it was the manly thing to do."

"Unless it was camouflaged?"

He grinned at her.

"The hospital has pads for things like that. Lieutenant Roker should have seen to it."

"I guess that sponge bath wasn't as exciting as she thought." He winked and Kate's insides clenched.

"I don't see how." Good grief, she thought. She was breathless just thinking about him wet and soapy and naked.

As if he could read her mind, his expression grew somber and heated.

Immediately, Kate sat down at the machine again, trying to catch her breath. He was her husband, for heaven's sake. It wasn't as if they hadn't had some exciting sex in the last few years, and right now she was feeling as if she'd just met him. She glanced at him as he sat in a nearby chair, then she continued sewing.

He was behaving a little differently. Ever since he'd had the stitches removed, his mood had changed, almost overnight. Kate couldn't be more pleased, because a grouchy Rick was no fun at all. But this man was just, well, more at ease. It made her wary. She was already weak for wanting him, and inside she was terrified that everything would go wrong and she'd get her heart broken once more. She didn't want the fantasy of being with him again to cloud her thoughts. But it was.

She sewed faster, the machine vibrating the table. Then, when she was satisfied with her work, she went to him, unlacing the sling and sliding into place the small pad that would protect the side of his throat and the back of his neck.

He stretched his head like an ostrich, testing it. "That's great, babe. I didn't realize how much it irritated till now."

"With the grump level at an all-time high, how could anyone tell?"

He gave her a sly look. "I'm not a grump."

"Of course not." She patted his head, then cleaned up her mess.

Rick moved as if to help with the machine, but when she eyed him pointedly, he sank back into the chair, enjoying watching her move around.

"Hungry?"

"God, no, after that breakfast? I bet I've gained a

If offer card is missing write to: Silhouette Reader Service, 3010 Walden Ave., P.O. Box 1867, Buffalo NY 14240-1867

NO POSTAGE
NECESSARY
IF MAILED
IN THE
UNITED STATES

BUSINESS REPLY MAIL

FIRST-CLASS MAIL   PERMIT NO. 717-003   BUFFALO, NY

POSTAGE WILL BE PAID BY ADDRESSEE

SILHOUETTE READER SERVICE
3010 WALDEN AVE
PO BOX 1867
BUFFALO NY 14240-9952

couple pounds already." He patted his stomach. Her gaze stopped there, and he felt heat charge through him when it traveled lower. Then, suddenly, she was looking around as if searching for something to do or, God help him, clean.

"You want to help me finish the window box?" he said abruptly.

She looked at him. "Using a saw? I don't know—"

"The wood is already cut. It just has to be assembled and sanded. I think with vise grips we can manage."

We. Kate was too pleased about this to balk at being around power tools.

"Sure." She grabbed a soda for each of them and they went into the garage. While he pulled out some planks of wood, Kate started some laundry and puttered.

"Come on, don't be afraid."

She thrust her chin up. "I'm not."

"Hell you aren't. Remember when you tried to hang a picture in the back hall?"

"Don't remind me, please." She'd swung the hammer so hard she'd missed the nail, smashed her finger and worse, put the hammer right through the wall. He'd teased her mercilessly for the two days it took him to repair her mistake. Kate acknowledged her limits after that.

Rick instructed her on how to clamp the planks in the vise to sand the edges, then together they worked to nail together and clean up the window box. It seemed like such a simple thing, her nailing as he held the wood, Rick teasing her not to nail his only working fingers to the board. Yet it gave her so much pleasure just to be near him without thinking about their problems.

It also made her aware of his scent, of the pure masculinity of him she'd fallen in love with. She glanced to the side, catching his eye, and suddenly remembered the moment she'd first seen him on a beach in California, near Camp Pendleton. It was such a lark, because she'd been living in Northern California at the time and was in the area attending a nursing conference in San Diego for a few days. Rick had been surfing, or as he later claimed, *learning* to surf, and her first glimpse of him was as he peeled off his neoprene wet suit and she got a load of that body. He'd looked at her, a stare so dark and powerful she'd stopped breathing.

Then he gave her that half-smile that still made her heart tumble in her chest, and although the Marines with him had started up a volleyball game, he'd ignored them and walked right up to her.

He'd introduced himself and asked if she wanted to take a walk. She wasn't about to go off with a stranger, and told him so. He'd promised to keep her in sight of her friends, but said that if they hung near his fellow Marines, she'd get a lesson in teasing and catcalls. By the time they'd walked a half mile down the beach she was sinking fast for him. He'd been so intense. In the way he looked at her, as if delving into her soul. He hung on her every word, his strength of character defined in so few of his own.

She was pretty much a goner even before he'd driven hours up the coast to surprise her. She'd been shocked to see him, and all he did was walk right up to her, take her in his arms and kiss her like no one had before.

Rick had always been a man of few words.

Was she trying to find what wasn't there? Did she want something from him he didn't know how to give?

"Earth to Kate."

"Hmm?" She dragged her gaze to his, smiling.

"You tired?"

"No, why?"

"You seem, I don't know, a little dazed."

"Just thinking."

"About what?"

"A beach in California."

His smile widened as he understood. "I still say it wasn't the bikini that got my attention."

"So it was the boobs falling out of my top?"

He gazed down at her, stroking her red hair off her face. "It was this." He rubbed a strand between his fingers. "Every man there wanted to get his hands in your hair. And on other parts, too."

She blushed. "And you're the exception?"

"No, I'm the only one who had the guts to go talk to you."

"Guts? Why?"

"Come on, babe, you're not that innocent, now. Men are intimidated by beautiful women. It's the rejection factor," he said.

"Ah, yes. Sort of like death before dishonor?"

"I wouldn't go that far." He handed her a piece of wood. "We can put this on the front in the center."

It was the Irish Claddagh symbol—of two hands, holding a heart. "It looks hand carved?" She turned it over in her hands.

"It is. Like I said, too many home and garden shows and too much time on my hands."

"*You* did it?"

His face reddened a bit as he nodded.

During their marriage, Rick had done lots of household stuff—the usual things, minor repairs and maintenance. But he'd spent his free time playing sports or working out. Or with her. He'd never been the hobby type.

But creating something new, out of raw materials, was more than just boredom, she thought, staring at the carving.

"It's beautiful, Rick! I'm amazed and, well, impressed. I knew you were handy with a knife, but you've never done anything like this before." The Irish emblem was perfectly carved on wood so thin she thought it would break. She carefully set it down. "Why the Claddagh?"

When he shrugged, she stepped near and met his gaze.

"You did it for me, didn't you?"

"Yeah."

Kate's heart tripped all over itself. "Why?"

"I was thinking about you at the time, I guess. You have that symbol everywhere." He tapped a finger on her silver Claddagh necklace.

She cupped the side of his jaw. "Thank you."

Rick swallowed, wondering what to do, what to say. She looked as if she was about to cry, and all he wanted to do was hold her. It wasn't right that he couldn't just do it, but he was afraid she'd pull back, and he didn't know if he could handle a cut like that.

Then he knew if he wanted her back he had to do what she needed: talk. He took a leap of faith and jumped. "I started carving that piece to get you out of my mind. I needed a distraction. All this was a distraction." He gestured to the wood and tools. "The harder I tried to ignore that you were gone, the more you haunted me," he said almost like a curse. "And just…"

He hesitated.

"And just what?"

"Just picturing you in this house, in our bed, made me feel as if I'd lost my entire world because I wouldn't talk."

Soft green eyes stared up at him. "You're talking now, Rick."

His gaze scored her upturned face and he stumbled over his thoughts and said, "I've really missed you, baby."

A tear spilled and rolled slowly down her cheek. The sight of it caught him in the chest like a well-placed hammer.

"Aw, Kate, honey." He slipped his good arm around her and she laid her head on his shoulder.

"I'll cherish this Claddagh, Rick," she muttered into his chest.

"It's just a silly window box."

"I know that. Oh, men are so stupid sometimes," she muttered tearily, and Rick thought, *We'll never get it.* How could something so trivial move her like this? Was it really that easy? Women. He'd never figure them out, least of all his own wife.

He pressed his lips to the top of her head for a moment, inhaling her perfume, then tipped her chin up.

She wet her lips, and it was all he needed. He captured her mouth and hunger exploded. Floodgates opened, pouring a torrential flood of desire and passion over him. Like a serpent it snaked through his blood, and she held on as his tongue plunged between her lips. He took control, devouring her, taking what he'd missed so much he'd thought he'd die. He needed her to breathe, to survive, and wanted her closer, cupping her round behind and pushing her into his erection, letting her know she had control.

But he wanted to be inside her, he pressed deeply, stroking her into the sweet madness and watching her pleasure erupt.

Then something hit the floor, and they parted, breathing heavily. He glanced at the screwdriver rolling across the concrete.

"Think that's a message to get busy?" he managed, smoothing one hand over her hair.

"I thought we were busy." Her teasing smile lit up the darkness inside him, pushing it aside.

He kissed her softly, delicately, this time, then said, "It won't look so good if we don't paint it."

She nodded, sniffling as she stepped back and focused.

"The Claddagh goes on last. Pick a color for the box." He showed her a number of unopened paint cans.

"Good Lord. Rick!"

He shrugged. "I couldn't decide."

She picked out a soft gold color for the box and a cream for the Claddagh, to blend with the house exterior, and he stirred while she wiped off the sawdust from their sanding.

"Where should we hang it?"

"I made it for the front, under the bay window in the living room." She agreed, and he watched her paint with small precise strokes.

"No one's going to look that close, Kate."

"I'll know."

"You are so ana—"

Her look stopped him from finishing the unattractive description. "Don't say it! I know. Drove my mother nuts."

"Everything is by the rules with you."

"Oh, look who's talking, Captain Spit and Polish, with his boots lined up in precise even rows."

"That's training."

"And who's going to inspect your gear in this house? At least my focused ways," she said before he could supply another word, "are a Zodiac thing. I'm a Scorpio. Nothing is ever as good as we think we can make it."

"Don't I know it."

She glanced up. "You're talking about us?"

"You want perfect."

"Nothing is ever perfect, least of all a marriage. I just want you to trust me enough to confide in me."

A little wall shot up in Rick's mind, blocking the pitiful past he'd tried hard to ignore. "You wouldn't want to hear it."

Her gaze narrowed. "Don't assume. Or would you like to test that theory right now?"

"I'm having fun, and since I've been bored silly for weeks now, let's not spoil it."

"Avoidance never solves a problem."

"Let's give it a try for today, huh?"

She eyed him for a couple of seconds, then conceded and went back to painting.

It was just plain interesting to watch her do even that.

Rick smiled to himself, loving the way her tongue rode her upper teeth in sync with the brushstrokes. His gaze swept her. Her ripe little body was wrapped in shorts and a tank top that fit snugly and outlined every delicious curve he wanted to possess. He swore she was wearing stuff like that just to raise his blood pressure. God knows it was reaching its limits this close to her. He wanted his hands on her, wanted to feel her grow wet and hot with the desire she kept locked up just for him.

He took a deep breath, shifting on the stool. This dangerous mind binge was not helping, he decided, and looked for something to do.

"Put your finger on this, will you?"

Kate snapped around to look as he started painting the Claddagh. "I can do that."

"I know, but I want to. Sort of like finishing my masterpiece." And not think about making love to her, he thought.

"Feels good to create something, huh?"

"Yeah. I never got to make anything when I was a kid unless it was in art class in school or shop class. When I was little I never had a backyard. Most of my foster homes were in apartments."

"You missed out on a lot. Brothers and sisters especially."

"I told you it wasn't heartwarming. And you fought with your siblings."

"What kids don't? Mom and Dad were referees most of the time."

"That's because guys don't want girl cooties."

She laughed shortly. "Yeah, my brothers would barricade themselves in a tree house and hoist the rope ladder so my sisters and I couldn't come up."

When Rick was done, she took the brushes to the utility sink to rinse them. "They always seemed to be having more fun than us."

"They were talking about bringing girls up there, and what they would do with them once they got them, trust me."

"They did. I caught Sean once."

Rick smiled, curious. "Doing what?"

"Making out."

"Learn anything?"

"Not anything you didn't show me," she blurted.

"I wasn't done."

She went still. Then her gaze jerked to his, his eyes gone smoky and piercing.

Kate felt riveted to the floor as he rose from the stool and moved toward her. Her heart did that double thump when he looked at her like that—as if he wanted to eat her alive. She'd enjoy every second of being devoured.

She licked her lips and he made a sound, of frustration and want. She recognized it. The same feelings were working their way through her right now.

"Dammit, Kate." He swept his arm around her, sandwiching her between the worktable and his long, lean body.

The brushes tumbled to the floor seconds before she put her hands on his chest. "This won't solve—"

"You're so sure?" He cut her off.

"No," she confessed.

"Neither am I."

His head dipped, his mouth swooping over hers. The crush of heat and hunger that had been building all day rippled through him and into her. She felt it, the tight muscles of his body, the long length of his thighs against hers. The need to wrap her legs around his hips made her arch into him, his kiss going wild and almost fanatical.

Her lips burned and his tongue slipped between, stroking her into madness.

"I want both hands on you."

Her own slid up and curved around his neck, and Rick moaned, feeling truly alive for the first time since she'd left. Heat pulsed through him in heavy waves, churning his blood and thickening his groin. He cupped her behind, pressing her to his hardness, letting her know just how she controlled this.

"I want to touch you again," he said against her lips. "There."

Kate moaned, her body on fire, her hand moving to his chest, nails circling his nipple. Rick felt longing rush through him, and opened her shorts, wanting to remind her how it was between them.

Then his hand dived inside, his finger sliding smoothly into her.

"Rick!" she cried, startled.

But then she relaxed as he moved in and out, circling the tender bead. He tortured her, loving the way her hips flexed and retreated, the way she gripped his shoulder. He kissed and kissed, sliding wetly, wishing he could open his jeans and bury himself inside her.

"Let it go, honey. Come on, I can tell you're so near. You can't hide it from me."

She was holding back, afraid to step into this part of their relationship again. Rick tried to understand it, knowing he'd have to win her back. Differently this time.

He introduced another finger, watched her eyes flare, felt her quicken with the coming explosion.

"Rick. Oh, it feels so good."

He smiled. She was leaning against the table, practically on it, one leg hooked around him.

It would be so easy to slide inside her, yet he dipped to her nipple, which was peaking against her tank top, and closed his mouth over it, wetting the fabric and sucking deeply.

She came unglued, and he experienced her pleasure—the shuddering gasps, the tiny moan of triumph as her body tightened down to her toes. The rush of heat and liquid warmth. It had always fascinated him, seeing her climax. It was never the same, never precise. She flowed with it, thrashing, leaning up to cup his face and devour his mouth.

Let him feel it, fusing and hot and passionate.

He held her tightly, kissing her until the fire simmered and faded.

"Oh. Rick."

"I love seeing you like that."

She blushed and pressed her head to his chest. "That was unfair, you know."

"I know. But I've missed you too much to apologize. And I won't."

Kate's throat burned with tears as she held on to him. She'd missed him, too—like breathing. Even while she slept she was reaching for him, and in the morning she was always wrapped around a body pillow. That emptiness was another reminder that her isolation was her own fault, and she squeezed him closer.

Rick tightened his own embrace, wishing for two good arms to hold the woman he loved.

So she'd never leave him again.

Seven

Rick winced as the glass slipped from his hand and hit the floor. He glanced over his shoulder, knowing Kate was out in the front yard planting flowers in the window box they'd made.

Hurriedly, he grabbed the broom and started sweeping up the mess. If she caught him without his sling, she'd read him the riot act in four languages.

The air was still crackling from their lovemaking in the garage, and though he wanted to take her to bed, he was literally an arm short. He didn't want to spoil it by screwing up.

He put his foot on the dustpan, sweeping the glass

up and hiding it in the bottom of the trash can. She'd been taking him to therapy and working with him to get his strength back, but she wanted him to go slow. Rick knew he was an impatient man and wanted it all done now.

When he heard the front door open, he quickly stashed the dustpan and grabbed a soda, trying to look nonchalant.

Then Kate came walking in, barefoot.

Oh hell. "Don't! Stop!"

She halted instantly, muddy hands in the air. "What?"

"I broke a glass," he confessed.

Her eyes narrowed and Rick knew that look. "And you don't have on the sling."

Oops. Immediately he put it back on.

She backtracked and slipped on sandals, then went for the broom and swept again. Then she mopped. Rick just watched her, shaking his head and accepting her uncompromising nature. Like she accepted his impatience.

"Don't push it with that arm, Rick, or you'll be sorry." She washed her hands and was about to give him another earful of her patience-is-a-virtue speech when the doorbell rang.

"Saved by the bell."

"Not hardly. I'll be watching you," she warned, then went to answer it. He followed.

Rick stood back. When she flung open the door, she shrieked and launched herself into a man's arms.

"Jace! Oh, I didn't know the advance party was back."

"What a shock, since you know everything."

The Marine Lieutenant set her back down, kissing her cheek, then lifting his gaze to Rick.

Rick smiled. "Get your hands off my wife, Marine."

Jace threw them up in the air. "Yes sir, Captain sir." Then he crossed to Rick, accepting his awkward handshake. "Man, you look great. I thought you'd be in the hospital still."

Kate moved between them, explaining that the only reason he wasn't was because she was a nurse.

"Lucky dog," Jace said with a glance at Rick. "I think I need to go out and get shot." Jace gave Kate a long, admiring look that set Rick's teeth on edge. He should be used to Jace's flirting with every woman he saw. The man had it down to an art form.

"Don't say that!" Kate gave him a playful shove.

"I wouldn't recommend it." Rick slung his good arm over Kate's shoulder. "She's a dictator."

Jace grinned at them.

"Hungry?" Kate asked.

"For your cooking? Yes, ma'am."

Kate smiled, glancing at Rick.

"What?" he said. "I can see something hatching in your mind."

"I was thinking that if the advance party is back that

means more men are hanging around on a Saturday, alone."

Rick doubted they were hanging anywhere, but said, "I'll make some calls."

"Nah, I will," Jace exclaimed, whipping out his cellphone. "It will cost you a beer, though."

Kate shook her head, heading for the kitchen and pulling out some steaks.

Jace was still on the phone when Rick handed him a beer. The last time he'd seen him, Jace had been beside the gurney, lifting him onto the evac chopper.

Jace tipped the phone away from his mouth for a second. "The place looks great, Rick."

Rick inclined his head toward Kate as she put potatoes and eggs on to boil.

Jace looked at her. "Figures."

"Do I have to beat you, Lieutenant?"

Jace grinned. "Like you could with that arm?"

"Stop looking at her like that."

"Then you shouldn't have married someone so pretty." Ending the call, Jace went to Kate, leaning against the counter. "Count four more, that okay?"

"Oh, sure."

"They're bringing beer and dessert."

"Good, because I wasn't planning on baking today."

"Santiago's fiancée is in town, too."

Kate glanced at Rick, smiling. "And here I thought

it was going to be me with six Marines. The testosterone level would have surely killed me."

Laughing, Rick came to her, standing behind her and sliding one arm around her as if staking his claim. It was the first time he'd been this close to her since the fun in the garage. He wanted more, wanted Kate naked and panting beneath him.

She glanced over her shoulder, touching his face, then said, "Why don't you two go outside? I have lots to do and you'll just be in the way."

"Sorry, we didn't mean for you to do all the work. We can call out for something, you know," Jace said.

"Take-out food after a six-month deployment? I *so* don't think so."

Rick knew she'd say that, and inclined his head to Jace. They went out to the back porch, and Kate got busy preparing potato salad and dragging out the partyware she'd bought just for get-togethers like this.

A half hour later the porch and yard were filled with single Marines relaxing and enjoying the day off before getting back to organizing the battalion. The advance party, a small group that always left a few weeks before the bulk of the troops to set up a mission command post, also came back to do the same before the rest returned. With her in the kitchen was Rachel, Gunnery Sergeant Mitch Santiago's fiancée. "You don't have to stay in here, Rachel. Go out there with Mac."

"And listen to all that Marine speak?" The pretty

blonde jutted her chin toward the backyard as she chopped vegetables. "They're talking shop and I still don't understand half of the abbreviations. PMO, TMO, BX, APC."

"Provost Marshal Office, Transportation Management Office, Base Exchange and Armored Personnel carrier," Kate said without thinking.

Rachel laughed. "How did you learn it all?"

She looked up, realizing how it rolled off so easily. "I had to learn it when Rick and I married." She shrugged. "Then more along the way. If you need to know anything, ask the Sergeant Major's wife." Kate told her the Marine Corps had actually developed a course, LINKS, to teach the lingo to Marine wives now. "We take care of our own."

"Well, I know *you* do."

Flattered, Kate put together some chips and dips and looked at Rachel. "We need to bust up that group and get them to talk about something else. Like your wedding?"

Rachel smiled. "I wish. I've been trying to get Mitch to decide on things for months."

"Well then, I'd say that's our mission?"

Rachel rushed to get her wedding planner and grabbed the dips, following Kate to the backyard.

The men stopped talking instantly and Kate knew they'd been discussing a mission that was classified. She whispered the same to Rachel as she set out the food, then looked at Mitch.

"Come on, Gunny, sit. You need to make some choices or you'll never walk down the aisle with Rachel."

Mitch smiled at his bride-to-be and came to her, kissing her softly. They were deep in a discussion when Jace said to Rick, "Your wedding was videotaped, right? She could watch it and see what a military wedding is like."

Rick looked at Kate, noting her startled expression. "I don't even know where it is," she murmured.

"I do," he said. She blinked up at him.

They moved into the house, and Rick went right to the tape and popped it into the player. Jace had been his best man, and as the couple sat on the sofa, the other Marines scattered around as Jace gave blow-by-blow comments. Rick and Kate stood back, watching the scenes unfold.

Her throat tightened as she saw herself meet Rick at the altar, how he took her hands in his and kissed the backs before the priest started speaking. She glanced at him. He was leaning against the wall, watching, then his gaze flicked to hers. Her eyes watered and Rick held out his arm to her. She came to him, sighing against his chest.

He dipped his head. "I watched this a lot after you left," he whispered.

She'd thought as much, since he knew where the tape was. "Why?"

"I was wondering how it started so great and ended so badly."

She held his gaze, stupid, silly tears blurring her vision. "Maybe because that was the last time I heard you say you loved me."

He groaned, squeezing her, and kissed her deeply, oblivious to Jace's comments, or the applause when, in the video, she and Rick ducked under the arch of swords and Jace whacked her on the behind, welcoming her into the Corps.

Sounds faded and Kate's fingers were in his hair, his mouth rolling over hers. Rick pulled her between his thighs, focused solely on her. "It's not over, Kate, you know that, don't you?" he said against her mouth, for her ears only.

"I don't want it to be."

He kissed her again with more power, as if doing so would brand her as he had on their wedding day.

Till someone said, "Jeez. Get a room, you two."

Rick pulled back, smiling over her head at the group. "I would if you guys weren't here."

Kate gathered herself together, feeling out of control with the kiss. Yet her mind snagged on his words. *It's not over.* But when he didn't need her help anymore, what then? When he recovered completely and was back in action, would that change? Revert to the way it had been?

And when she told him of the child she'd lost? She

looked up at him for a long moment, scared inside, then turned her attention to their guests. "Who's ready for chow?"

"Oh no, you don't, Marine," Kate said, coming into the garage like an F-18 jet at Mach 1.

Rick was on the exercise machine that was as big as a car, which was why it was in the garage. The instant the stitches were out, his mood had changed. He envisioned his recovery coming a little closer. That was great, but it meant she had to watch him. He'd overdo it because he was impatient. Being up at the crack of dawn and sneaking a workout proved it.

"You heard the doctor. It's too soon for that much weight. Get off that machine and put this on."

She shoved the sling at him, trying not to notice how sexy he looked bare chested, wearing nothing but black shorts. The muscles of his thighs flexed with power as he pushed on the pedestal, bringing an unbelievable amount of weights up the pulley system behind him.

He shook his head. "It'll get dirty."

"I'll wash it. Stop. Now, Rick."

He let the weight down and took the sling. "I'm done, anyway."

She smothered a shriek and whirled back into the house.

Rick smiled to himself and grabbed a towel, wiping down. He'd left the sling in the bathroom on purpose, knowing she'd come charging after him. She was spending way too much time cleaning stuff that didn't need to be cleaned, to avoid him. For a woman who'd been in his face twenty-four–seven for three weeks, she had made herself scarce in the last couple of days.

He knew exactly why.

They'd gotten past the uncomfortable newness of being together again. Her barking orders, him obeying them because, well, she wouldn't give him a choice. All she had to do was brush past him, touch him, even in a medical manner, and he was lit up like a firecracker. And so was she. Even looking at her across the dinner table was tough because he could remember how many times dinner went cold while they'd made love—all over the house.

He scented her like a stag, his body so aware of her that his heartbeat thumped like a hammer. Yet now that he wasn't covered in bandages, the tension between them grew to abominable heights. He could move more, and he was making good use of the mobility.

When he entered the kitchen, she was slamming cabinet doors and moving around without accomplishing anything.

"It's way too early for this, Kate. Calm down."

"I knew you would do this."

"It was just some leg presses."

"Without a spotter. You weren't supposed to—" She clamped her lips shut and closed the cabinet so carefully Rick could feel her fighting her temper.

He tried to adjust the sling straps and she moved closer, helping him. It was exactly what he wanted. Her, closer.

"I'm going to glue that sling on you. You can take it off when you sleep if you prop up the cast." She shook her head, adjusting the straps for him. Her face was inches from his as she reached around. "I swear, Rick, you're so stubborn."

"Look who's talking, Irish."

Her gaze flashed up, and in her eyes Rick saw that she remembered. Remembered how it was between them, the heat and passion, the ravenous need for each other. And that that was when he called her Irish.

A nervous little smile curved her lips. "Work out only the legs, okay? No sit-ups."

Rick couldn't if he tried. It put too much strain on his shoulders. He wanted his energy for other things. "If I don't do something, I'm going to get fat and sloppy."

Kate's gaze moved over him. "Not a chance." He was used to running every day. A body like Rick's didn't happen overnight.

When she started to move away, he snapped his arm around her waist and pulled her close.

"Ew, Rick, you're sweaty." Her hand splayed over

his chest and all she wanted to do was burrow into his arms.

Rick felt gut punched from the need pouring through him. "Get sweaty with me."

"I don't even know how to use that machine."

His voice was whiskey rough as he said, "I didn't mean with the equipment."

She stared owlishly, and before she could think, he'd backed her up against the island counter.

"Rick."

"I've missed touching you," he said softly. He cupped her jaw. "Every time I look at you I remember what you taste like, what it feels like to be inside you. You're driving me crazy." His gaze slipped over the short satiny nightgown and robe, her hair tossed from sleep. There was a lushness about her that humbled him.

"I don't mean to." Giddy pleasure swept through her as she stared up at him.

"Honey, you don't even have to try."

His free hand roamed her shoulder, dribbling down her breasts, pausing to tease and stroke, and her breath came faster. But Kate didn't stop him. She wanted his touch. Months without him had been like losing a limb, had robbed her of feeling anything except the loss of him in her life.

He took her mouth like he owned it, like he was dying for her, his hand slipping under her nightgown to her naked behind. Warm and seeking.

And she devoured him back, a wet slide of lips and tongue that pulsed with hunger.

Rick thought he would disintegrate right then, a year's worth of need crashing through him in hot liquid waves. She moaned deeply, and he cupped her center, rubbing.

"Rick," she said against his mouth. A meager protest, she knew. Being near him was turning into torture, till she welcomed sleep only to have him appear in her dreams, reminding her of the passion they'd shared. Yet dreams never satisfied, leaving her wanting him so badly hunger struck like a slap, and nursing him was the last thing on her mind.

"I want to touch you again, baby. I need to." Under her nightgown, he palmed her bare skin still warm from sleep, and her kiss grew hungrier, a message Rick wouldn't ignore. Her heat pressed to his erection sheathed in dark cloth, searing him.

He throbbed for her.

She'd have to be numb not to know it. Kate did.

It fueled what was already there, bringing awareness to an overpowering level. And her will, her misgivings, slipped from her grasp, her desire filling the space and reminding her that he was still *hers*. She knew this wouldn't fix anything, but he'd been the last man to touch her body and the only one to touch her soul. Rick made it so enjoyable to be female, she thought as his hand slid to her shoulders, pushing the robe off. The satiny fabric whispered to the floor as he hooked her straps and pulled them down.

Kate couldn't move, couldn't speak, the heat in his eyes imprisoning her where she stood. He dragged the fabric low, letting it tease her breasts as he leaned in. He met her gaze for a second, then wrapped his lips around her nipple.

A bolt of heat spiraled through her like a pulse sonar, her head dropped back and she arched, offering herself. And he took, devouring her with a desperation that drove all thought from her brain.

Throbbing pleasure pricked her skin.

His nearness was like a drug, teasing her with the addiction.

His teeth nipped at her rib cage, her waist as he pushed the nightgown to the floor. It pooled silently as his mouth moved lower, boiling the blood racing beneath her skin. Then his fingers teased her center, making her flex.

"Rick," she gasped.

"Want me to stop?" His finger dipped and her breath shuddered.

"No."

He kissed her deeply, then slipped his arm under her rear and lifted her onto the counter.

"Rick!" He would hurt himself.

He didn't seem to care, stripping off the sling, then immediately wedging himself between her thighs. He drew her against him, letting her feel his arousal.

"I've been this way since you walked through the door." He kissed her thickly, his hand mapping her body, spreading her thighs wider. "I've been just *existing* without you, Kate."

"Oh, Rick."

She shouldn't. She really shouldn't. This wasn't going to help anything except the desire flooding through her. But being with Rick like this again made her lose all reason. She moaned and her insides clenched, warming with wet heat, her hips pushing on the demanding hardness between them.

"You taste so good, better than before."

She laughed softly.

And Rick feasted, ravenous for the taste of her. He nibbled and kissed, sucked until a luxurious moan spilled from her lips. He caressed her contours, loving her curves, his fingers brushing over her center, teasing her.

"Touch me, Rick," she whispered in his ear, and he felt unhinged. "I want to feel you inside me."

His fingers stroked over her hot center, a rush of honeyed heat answering him. Her scent drove him mad with want, and he slid one finger inside her—slowly, watching her shudder and arch.

"That feels so good." Her hips rocked and he introduced another finger, pushing deeply, then withdrawing, hearing her breath catch with the motion.

"I want to taste you, all of you. Show it to me,

honey. I know you're close." Just to taunt her, he pushed inside slowly and withdrew with equal patience. Her entire body quivered under his touch.

He pushed her back, bending. "Do you remember when we did this the first time in here?"

"Yeah."

"And the second?"

"Why are you talking *now?*"

He chuckled and leaned forward, tasting the joint of her thigh. She was breathing hard, her body tense. Rick knew this woman, what she liked, and he tempered his need for her. "Outside at midnight under the stars?"

The memory flashed through her brain. "Oh, yeah." It had been so erotic, so decadent, the threat of being caught heightening their senses.

"I want that heat." He dipped his head and covered her softness.

She shrieked and laughed, throwing her head back. He cupped her buttocks, holding her for his assault, and brought her closer to rapture, her hips rolling in a sensuous wave with each stroke of his tongue. Kate was always vocal and this time was no exception. She whispered that her toes curled when he did that, that her heart was in her throat. That her body was his.

Then she didn't have to tell him anything more.

He knew.

Her spine curved, her sculptured body flexed. Then

she found it, and stiffened, shivered delicately, calling
his name and begging for him to push inside her. He
didn't, and an incredible feeling washed over him as
he watched her pleasure erupt, felt it, tasted it. She was
a wild creature trapped in the throes of her own passion. He didn't want it to fade, wanted to experience
it with her again and again, smiling at her mewling
cries of pleasure even when she was spent and panting.

She collapsed, melting. Rick swept his hand over
her body, laid bare for him.

"Oh, Rick." She rose up and reached for him.

He went still, his eyes intense as he suddenly experienced the enormity of the moment. She was in his
arms, wanting him as badly as he did her, but he realized he'd let their marriage take second place, like a
misplaced toy, and it wasn't going to come back with
simply being found again. He hadn't a clue how to give
her what she needed. Except this way.

Her fingers on his jaw brought him back, and he
kissed her softly, then pulled her off the counter, letting her fall against him.

Kate stepped away, taking his hand, tugging him
with her toward their bedroom.

He stopped and she looked back. "Don't ask me if
I'm sure, Rick."

"I won't," he said, drawing her into his arms, his
hands everywhere. He could barely breathe with

wanting her so much, and backed her toward the doorway.

Kate plunged her hand inside his shorts, sweeping around to cup his tight behind. He ground himself against her, then staggered to the bedroom. Falling back on the bed, he smiled up at her, and was surprised he felt a little nervous.

She was like a gift he'd seen, unopened, knowing it was for him, but denied the thrill of discovering what was inside. And now he could.

Eight

Kate hovered over him, naked and beautiful, and his throat tightened. His fingers sank into her hair and he cupped her face, trapped in her liquid green eyes.

"Don't talk. Don't question. Please, baby. We should, right now."

She smiled. "I was just wondering if you have any protection?" As she spoke she pushed the dark shorts down, inching back enough to flick them off. Her gaze slid over his body like honey.

Leaning forward, she opened the nightstand drawer and found the condoms right where they'd left them, untouched. Grabbing one, she met his gaze, climbing to straddle his thighs.

"I'm not gonna last," he groaned.

His back against a mound of pillows, Rick watched her slither sexily on top of him, peeling open the little packet. He flinched wildly when she enfolded him, obviously taking pleasure in sheathing him.

"You're killing me!"

She just grinned, sliding warmly on him, teasing him. Rick squeezed his eyes shut at the sensations burning through him like fire.

"Kate, honey. I want to see you remember." He thrust upward, cupping her face, his gaze locked with hers as he filled her.

His throat burned. She'd kept such a distance between them lately, and he wanted her to remember it all, miss nothing. He gripped her hips, giving her motion, and absorbed her like fresh rain, feeling the broken bond reforge.

Her body sang, calling to him, and he thrust again, entranced by her expression.

She chanted his name, her hips pumping wildly. Rick clutched her and watched her explode, her hips shoving, then her mouth ravenous on his. She was vocal and animated.

He loved that about her. It excited him, how sexy and untamed she was. For him. Only him.

His shoulder throbbed from the effort it took to keep from gripping her with his wounded hand as she pushed against him.

"Rick. Rick."

"Look at me. Now." She obeyed, cupping his face in her palms, her eyes hazy, her body pulsing as he pushed deeper, harder. Her panting undid him; the pawing of her feminine muscles around him drove him wild.

Rapture hovered, then fractured. She cried out, clinging, kissing him. Pain and passion blended as he stared into her eyes, felt his climax claw up his body and demanding his attention. He thrust, then withdrew slowly, then plunged again into her hot tight haven.

The summit beckoned.

Fiery ecstasy climbing.

She buried her face in his chest and held on tight. "Rick."

"I know, baby. I know."

The ride continued with his heavy length pulsing inside her, touching her womb. Then Kate came apart and he bucked, his hand stroking her tender nub.

"I want you to remember this, baby. Never forget this."

Tears seared her eyes. "I never did, Rick. Never."

She loved him: she'd never stopped. As the crest of desire peaked and shattered over them, Rick felt the depth of his loss, the love he'd hadn't cherished enough, hadn't held on to. Ecstasy filled him, along with despair.

* * *

Kate woke before Rick. The last hours had been a physical strain for him, she knew. He hadn't done so much as move from bed to chair since the surgery.

She sat back on her calves, watching him sleep, thinking he was the best-looking thing on the planet— and that she'd probably made a big mistake by forgetting their problems and making love to him.

Yet she felt complete, the missing part of herself back where it belonged.

Nothing was resolved, except they were physically close once more. Not that she was complaining. Just looking at him made her want him again. But she knew she had to dump some of her perfectionist attitude, and not push him so hard to talk. Perhaps she'd have to face the fact that Rick would never share parts of himself, while she shared everything.

Well, not everything, she thought, her heart clenching as she remembered their baby, of being so alone when she'd lost it, and wanting to tell him. To be held and comforted by him. He'd been out of the country on some mission, she knew; they wouldn't contact him or tell her where he was.

Telling him about their child was still a block between them. She couldn't bring herself to do it yet. Everything was so fragile....

"Hi," he said.

She met his gaze, and he smiled sleepily, reaching

to run his hand over her bare hip. "Every man's fantasy is to wake up with a beautiful naked woman beside him."

"Good afternoon." She glanced at the clock. "Or should I say evening."

"Time flies." He wiggled his brows.

"Hungry?"

"Yes. Starved. But I have a better plan."

He pulled her down on him, his hands mapping her naked spine. He kissed her slowly, then met her gaze.

"I know, baby, you don't have to say it. Here, we're great. It's out there we have trouble."

"You didn't think we did."

"I'm seeing it a little differently now."

She smiled, being content with that for the moment. She kissed him, working her way down his throat, his chest, then tenderly she kissed his wound.

"I'll heal by tomorrow for sure."

She laughed lightly, snaking her tongue over his nipple. His breath sucked in hard. She was sliding down his body, laying wet sultry kisses across his flat stomach, when the doorbell rang.

She looked up.

"Great," he said. "Someone has lousy timing."

Kate rose up, searching the covers. "Where's my robe?"

"In a puddle on the kitchen floor," he said, rolling off the bed, grabbing a pair of jeans and pulling them on. "Sit tight, I'll get it. You're not answering the door looking like that."

His gaze melted over her and Kate smiled. "Naked?"

"Freshly loved." Rick winked. He walked out, already too damn hard to appear before visitors.

Kate searched for something to put on and slipped into one of his worn Recon T-shirts. She was still sitting on the bed when he came back, holding an envelope and a stack of papers. It was his expression that caught her in the chest.

He lifted his gaze. He looked so wounded. Hurt.

"Rick, what's the matter?"

He didn't say anything as he dropped the papers on the bed between them.

Kate frowned, snatching them up. She didn't have to read past the heading. It was the divorce papers.

"I didn't know you'd filed."

"I didn't. The attorney must have done it after a year of no contest."

Rick's features pulled taut. It was as much his fault. He'd never contested, just agreed and went along. He had no one to blame but himself.

His gaze stayed locked on the tattered manila envelope. "Papers, hell." He sat on the bed and rubbed his face. "I suddenly feel like a kid."

"A kid? Why?"

He was quiet, not saying anything, and Kate slipped

from the bed, convinced that he wouldn't. Little pricks of pain tortured her with his silence. It was so like before, where he'd just shut her out.

Then he spoke, and she looked at him sharply.

"When I was a kid, everywhere I went in the foster system I came with papers." He gestured to them. "One beat-up bag, and papers telling them who I was and some report from a social worker. People didn't even talk to me, they just read the papers and shuffled me in or out. I think it's why I hate writing fitness reports on my men. How can you tell who a person is from a two-paragraph summary?"

"You can't."

"Well, they did. I didn't have such great reports, either. I read one when I was about fifteen. Antisocial, unruly, refuses to talk."

It was the first time he'd revealed anything like this, anything deeper than just the vague summaries he disliked. Kate took each word as a little treasure.

"It didn't matter."

"Yes, it does. Don't tell me it's not important, because you haven't gotten past it." She moved beside him, making him look at her, and she was struck with the haunted expression in his eyes just then. "I'm not afraid to hear it."

"I am."

"Why? It's part of who you are."

"No it's not!" He stood abruptly. "I worked hard to

get out of that hellhole and I've come too far to look back." She couldn't handle it, he thought. He had to be the strong one. He had to carry the ugliness of his past and his career. She was so loving and gentle-hearted that he knew hearing the details would destroy that innocence he loved about her. She'd come from a big loving family and had no idea what it had been like. Besides, he was over it, had dealt with it in his own way.

Rick sighed, rubbing his face and thinking this was exactly why there were divorce papers sitting on the bed between them.

"Looking back is not the same as *going* back. I have things in my life I don't want to examine, either. But they've made me who I am right now," she argued.

"Oh, yeah? What things? Being cut from the cheer-leading team? Beaned your brother with a rock when you were in the third grade? How about not knowing your real name till you were six?"

Her eyes flew wide and she stepped back in shock.

Rick saw it, felt it cut into him, and if he needed proof that she'd react like the last woman he'd con-fessed to, he had it.

He left her without a word, and Kate sank slowly to the bed, the tangle of sheets still warm from their bod-ies. There was more to his experience than he'd ever let on, and she hopped off the bed and chased after him. She found him on the back porch, staring out at the pool.

"You can't leave it at that, Rick."

"Wasn't that enough?"

She grabbed his good arm, forcing him around only because he let her. Then she moved in closer, touching the side of his face. "I don't know what holds you back every time, but you have to trust me."

"What holds me back is that the last woman I told about how I was raised disappeared real quick."

Kate stepped back. "Don't insult me by comparing me to some woman you never mentioned before."

He looked above her, staring at nothing for a long moment. "I've made a lot of mistakes, Kate. I know that."

"Yes, you have. So have I. How about you stop trying to hide everything from me? I'm stronger than I look."

His eyes were hooded, so solitary her heart ached. She'd left him, so what made her think he'd believe her? Regret swept her and she tried another tack.

"You know, Rick, I knew who you were when I married you. I knew what being married to a Marine entailed. I didn't walk in blindly. Have I ever been a bad Marine wife?"

"No, of course not." She was the best, he thought, keeping their life in line and marching on while he vanished for months at a time.

"Then why do you expect me to react like that witch?"

He let out a long, tired breath and stared at the rippling water of the pool. "I didn't want to risk losing you by telling you all of it. Can't you see that?"

"I do now. But you *didn't* tell me."

"And you left, anyway."

Her face flamed. "I said I made mistakes. But you didn't come after me, Rick. That spoke really loud."

"I did."

Her features went taut. "What?"

"I did go after you. A day later. I went to the hospital. I was outside the E.R. You were working, and smiling at everyone, and I thought, I'm dying inside and she's fine without me."

"Damn it, Rick, you should have come talk to me. Those smiles were for show, for the patients. I wasn't fine." She'd kept it all in, hoping he'd come for her.

He turned his head, met her gaze. "You're right, I just accepted it."

Because everyone had left him in the past, she thought. Why would he expect otherwise?

"I figured you just couldn't handle military life, being alone all the time, doing everything." And didn't love me enough to hang around and try, he added silently.

"I did and you know it, dammit. You didn't trust me or *us*."

"No, I didn't," he admitted. "I knew I'd sent you away, Kate."

"You *pushed* me away. Don't you think we have a chance now?"

He looked at her with such hope in his eyes her stomach clenched. But he only nodded.

She swallowed hard, then ventured to say, "How is it that you didn't know your name?"

Rick was quiet for a moment, his brow knitting. "I was three or four when I was abandoned into the system. I didn't have any records, but the cops tried to find my mother. It took awhile, but they did. She was dead." His shoulders moved as if shrugging off the pain of a child. "Drugs, I think. I don't know. Nor do I care. But before they found her, I was entered into a computer, with reports. Some clerk simply typed in something and I suddenly had a new name. It wasn't until they located my birth certificate that I learned my name was Richard Wyatt. Before that I was Johnny, John Smith, John no one, whatever."

She pulled him down to the wicker porch sofa, sitting beside him, her heart breaking for the little boy no one wanted. He kept staring out at the yard.

"Thanks for telling me that much, but how rough you had it isn't the point, Rick. It's part of who you are, but not the man you are now. What matters is that you think you have to keep everything inside and not talk about it that hurts you. You lost men and didn't talk to me, or anyone. I hurt when you hurt, Rick. But

I know now that you don't want to tell me everything, and I won't push anymore."

It was the resolute tone that made him look at her. "Yeah, right, you're the pushiest woman I know."

She sighed, laying her head on his shoulder. "It's the Irish in me."

"It's what I loved about you."

Loved. Past tense again. Kate's heart tore in half and she wondered if her pestering had ruined everything between them.

"You see everyone as good, Kate, before you see the bad. Even then you won't face it."

"You make me sound like a first-class sap."

Smiling, he threw his arm around her and pressed his lips to her temple. "No, it's innocence, a trusting nature." He looked down, tipping her chin up. "I adore that in you. Your energy. The room is a little brighter when you walk in."

A lump swelled in her throat and her eyes teared up. He leaned forward and kissed her softly.

"I need that," he whispered against her lips. "I need that so badly."

She was a bright star, and Rick felt as if he cut her off at the knees every time he didn't talk things out with her. He admitted it was harder to *not* talk than talk. "I didn't want to spoil it, Kate. And I did, didn't I?" He thought of the divorce papers in the bedroom, like a snake about to strike.

"No." She leaned to kiss him. "No."

She'd been shocked by his statement, the pain in his tone slicing through her soul. This little bit of his past told her there was more. Oh, she knew about his uncle, that when they'd found he had a living relative, the welfare system had brought him to his mother's brother. Rick rarely said more, dropping only vague pieces of information over the years. His past wasn't what had made her fall in love with him four years ago.

It wasn't a weakness.

It was his strength.

This ability to grow beyond his troubled past. He'd gone to college on scholarships, been selected for Officer Candidate School, graduated number one and was instantly selected for Force Recon. That said a lot about a boy who'd been abandoned with nothing but the clothes on his back and no one to love him.

Everyone had abandoned Rick at some point. Foster parents, his unfeeling uncle. And now her.

Shame and regret welled through her, because when she'd left he'd probably expected it, so he didn't fight. It hurt that he hadn't bothered to chase after her, but in the past days, she'd come to understand that Rick might be an iron man on the outside, the tough, strong man he showed the world, but inside he felt like the kid who'd been shuffled around with a stack of papers.

When it came to fighting for love, he didn't know how. Because no one ever fought for *his* love.

She was trying. "I had a hand in it, too. And I'm sorry."

Rick stared down at her, his broad hand enfolding her delicate jaw. Just looking at her made his hope flare and he decided that if they were on their way back, it was going to be different this time. It had to be—he wasn't going to lose her again. He'd die before he let that happen.

Then he kissed her softly and whispered, "Me, too, baby. Me, too."

A few days later, the stationary pins were removed. Rick swore the process was worse than being shot, and while there would always be a couple of pins in his wrist, the doctor declared that his bones were knitting well. He felt almost bionic, but before he could get excited about being out of the cast, they put another one on. This one didn't restrict his fingers so much and was lighter, the weight no longer pulling on his tender shoulder.

While Kate was off running some errand, Rick worked to regain his strength. She'd go bezerk if she knew he was doing exercises. But impatience was his worst enemy. He had a few days before the battalion returned and he wanted to be in uniform for the occasion.

He set the fist grip down, looking around the kitchen. Then he started to drag out pots and pans, practically clueless as to what he was doing. But he wanted to give Kate a break. She'd been working like a madwoman, feeding him so much he'd gained weight. If he hadn't appreciated his wife before, he did now. She'd worked a full-time job, and could manage more in a day than his whole company. Being around her, he saw what she did to make their house a home—noticed she'd brought in flowers and put up pictures. She was moving in with him again, he thought. Rick opened the fridge, wondering what he could manage to cook without blowing up the house.

An hour later, Kate returned home and rushed into the kitchen, waving her hand in front of her face and wincing at the shriek of the fire alarm. She grabbed a cookie pan and waved the smoke from the fire sensor.

When they went off she heard him say "thank God," and she laughed. He spun around, looking guilty. And ridiculous in the cobbler's apron.

"What are you doing?"

"Making a mess, can't you tell?"

She walked closer, noticing the very nice salad in the bowl, then the broiler with something shriveled and burned in the center of it.

"I know it doesn't look like it, but I started off with good intentions." He shook his head sadly.

She peered, trying not to laugh. "Chicken?"

"It was. I think an arson squad will determine how it ended up like this."

She laughed softly and looked up at him. "Why are you doing this?"

"You've been working so hard, and well," he shrugged, almost bashful, "I wanted to give you a break."

She glanced at the mess. "Take-out would have been a break." She met his gaze again.

"What's the matter? It's not that bad, is it?" She looked as if she was about to cry.

"This is so sweet, Rick." Kate was touched beyond measure. "I can see the cast wasn't what was really stopping you from cooking."

"Obviously I'm the one who lacks this talent in the family."

Family. Kate felt suddenly stung again with the fact that she hadn't told him about the baby she'd lost.

"MREs are so much easier." He tossed the burned food in the trash and set the broiler pan in the sink. "Kelly dropped by to get the other containers, by the way. The guys come back in a few days."

"You're excited."

"Yeah, just need some news." He went to the stove, stirring something.

"Been pretty boring here, huh?"

He glanced at her, his velvety gaze sweeping lazily

over her from head to toe, making her remember the last time they'd made love, wild and outrageous in the tub. "I wouldn't say that."

She stepped close, peering in the pot. "And this is?"

"Fettuccini Alfredo."

"Really?"

"That's what the Sergeant Major's wife said."

"Bet that's not all," Kate muttered, heading to the phone and dialing, holding a finger up when he started to ask. Then she ordered an entrée from a local restaurant.

"I'd rather take you out."

"Not with your fingers swelling like that."

He looked at his hand, then frowned. They were a little puffy.

Rick expected her to rant at him, but instead she went to the freezer, pulled out an ice pack and ordered him to sit. He obeyed, and she packed his arm in ice.

"No tirade?"

"Would it do any good? You're paying for your crime right now, Marine."

"Where did you go?" he asked when she started cleaning up the mess.

"To get some more clothes."

He frowned, adjusting the pack. God, his hand was throbbing. "Where do you live?"

She looked up. "I was wondering when you'd ask that."

Rick felt a stab of shame. Another fact he hadn't bothered to learn. "Well?"

"I have a one bedroom apartment about a mile from here."

A mile? She'd been that close and he didn't know it? Rick rubbed his forehead, thinking what an ass he'd been. "I'm sorry. I don't know why I never asked."

"You just didn't want to acknowledge I was still near, Rick," she said, her voice fracturing a little.

"I didn't. I kept thinking you'd come back."

She stared at him over the counter. "We're a team. Your missions are classified, not your feelings. When you hurt, I feel it. Don't you understand that? You're not alone."

"I was never sure about telling you any of it, Kate. I guess I felt that if you saw the worry, then you'd be afraid, and I didn't want to leave you like that every time I deployed."

"Oh, give me a break. It's not like I don't have tons of people to talk to—the other wives, my family. My friends to turn to. I'm a damn good Marine wife and I'm perfectly capable of handling anything, and you know it."

"I've seen a lot of ugly things, and I didn't want to lose that way you looked at me."

"What way?"

"I don't know, it's sorta…" He stopped, and Kate walked over to him.

"Hero worship?"

He made a face. "Nah. Like I was special."

She had a feeling he didn't mean in a loving way, but something else. "Special how?"

He slipped his arm around her, pulling her between his thighs. "Like I was good enough for you."

"Oh, Rick." She sat on his knee, gazing into his eyes. "I wouldn't have fallen in love with you if you weren't. And you don't have to be so inflexible, either. I never expected that of you. You did that to yourself."

"And I lost you, anyway."

She blinked. "After the past few weeks, you really think that?"

"You were divorcing me." His tone was bitter with hurt.

She stood and Rick frowned, following right on her heels. The papers were in the bedroom, like a sore that wouldn't close. Kate marched in there and picked them up.

Then she went to the fireplace and set a match to them, tossing them in. She watched them flame, while he moved up behind her.

Rick was still as glass, so silent he could hear his own pulse. "Kate…"

She looked up. "We aren't there yet, Rick."

"Thank God." He gathered her in his arms and kissed her deeply, with a gentle tenderness that melted her bones.

Nine

Rick woke abruptly, sweating. He sat up, bracing his back against the headboard, and stared into the dark.

His gaze shifted to where Kate lay beside him. Even after they'd started making love again, she'd slept in the other room, yet tonight she'd ended up here. He cherished the fact, watching her sleep. When he swiped at the dampness on his forehead, she stirred, rolling over and blinking sleepily.

"Nightmare?"

"Not really, just a rehash of it all." His bad dreams had eased over the past weeks, giving him an analytical perspective instead of having him in the midst of turmoil.

She shifted, gathering the sheet to her breast, and he leaned over, kissing her, smoothing her hair back. She looked so much like a little elf sitting there that he smiled.

"I know it's pointless to ask, but—"

He eased back, holding her gaze for a long moment, then sighed and said, "We were in the hills outside Kandahar."

Kate held her breath, as if she were about to leap into the unknown.

"It's cold there now. Wind howls like crazy through the mountains. We were to dispatch a group of rebels in the hills. We had them surrounded and they panicked, firing blindly. I had two teams forward. They were supposed to get inside the caves and draw them out. I was covering them with my team."

Kate listened to him, not so much his account of the ambush, which had come from behind, but how he told it. In between details he related what he'd felt, heard, not just the mission report he'd give his commander. She listened about how he'd been hit by a sniper and crawled out into the open to eliminate the threat to his men.

"Never thought I'd seen anything so wonderful as that corpsman hovering over me."

He stared at his fists the whole time he talked, and then he lifted his gaze to meet hers. His voice was solemn as he said, "I thought of you, Kate, only you. I knew that even if you weren't in this house, you were somewhere safe, and that was good enough for me."

Kate felt the ache in his words.

"I kept telling myself I'd find you as soon as I could. That I wouldn't waste time, and I'd make you come back." He grasped her hand, holding it to his chest. "Then here you were, never too far away."

Kate's lips trembled and she inched closer, kissing him and whispering a teary, "Thank you."

She knew she should tell him about their baby right now. But she felt as if they were still walking on eggshells that were about to crack. Just because they'd crossed a bridge didn't mean everything was fine.

She wanted a big family and he didn't. How they'd managed to avoid bringing up the subject in the past weeks was a work of art in evasion. Rick had grown up without anyone around and didn't know how much fun it was having brothers and sisters. He didn't even want one child. And he hadn't wanted that close tie to anyone, she knew. Yet when he scooped her onto his lap, smiling at her, all thoughts of anything but him vanished.

She shifted, straddling his thighs.

Instantly his hand went under her nightgown. "You're so warm and soft." He stroked the curves of her behind, then palmed her breasts. She tipped her head back, covering his hands with hers.

"I love when you touch me."

"I want you again."

"Really? I wouldn't know." She ground against his hardness under the sheets, then reached between them, grasping him.

"Kate." He said it with a groan.

"Now, Rick. I want you, now."

He stripped the nightgown off over her head, the idea of having her pulsing through him like a thunderbolt. He pulled her closer, his tongue laving her nipple, feeling it peak beneath his touch.

He slipped his hand between her thighs, spreading her, positioning, and Kate thrust against him. He filled her hotly, eliciting a long moan from her, and she was on him like a wild creature, kissing him, retreating, then thrusting her hips and taking him away from their problems.

She was untamed, in control, and he let her have it.

"Rick."

"Come on, honey. Don't stop. Whatever you want, I'm game for it." He wanted her energy, wanted to give her everything she needed because she gave every part of herself to him.

He regretted not cherishing it, thinking he didn't deserve her, but Rick understood, finally, that Kate was meant to be his. She'd been trying to tell him that, in her own way. He just hadn't listened very well. She needed him to need her. He did, like breathing, but he'd never told her, never spoke the simple words that would have kept her with him and given her what she wanted. It was so little to ask.

She cupped his face, her gaze locked with his as she rode him passionately. She begged for more, shivering in his arms, going tense and tight, rocking wildly.

He'd never seen anything so beautiful as her climax, the expression on her face, the glazed look in her eyes. He watched her release shatter through her and it sent him over the edge. The coarse hardness of his passion erupted, a storm pulsing with their tempo, and he thrust upward, his arms clamped tightly around her, their bodies fused with energy and pleasure.

He choked on the emotions bombarding him and ran his hand up her spine, feeling her shimmer in his arms.

Then softly, like a flower spent for the season, she collapsed.

Rick didn't let her go, the silence of the night coating them.

He loved her. More than anything in his life.

Now he had to find a way to prove it.

Visitors were starting to stop by.

It was something Rick hadn't really thought about until it began. Whether he or Kate wanted to think that no one knew they'd been apart, this told him the truth. They all knew.

They hadn't come to seek her out before, either

knowing she wasn't here, or not wanting to intrude. But the trickle of visitors had become a constant influx in the last couple of days, because the battalion was returning. Families were gearing up for the landing.

Rick was eating a quick sandwich when Kate went to answer the door. The sound of excited voices drew him out of the kitchen, and he found her with a blond woman who looked familiar. Kate was holding a small bundle.

"Rick, you remember Tina? Staff Sergeant Ridge's wife?"

He nodded, greeting her.

"And this—" Kate pulled back a blanket to reveal a tiny baby "—is Emma."

Rick moved close, staring down at the beautiful infant. "She's so small."

"Makes it better for giving birth," Tina said. "Want to hold her?"

"Oh, hell, no." He backed away, but something in Kate's expression tightened his gut. "I don't know the first thing about babies."

"Hold her like a football," Tina said.

Rick flapped his arms. "My football arm is broken." He was saved when another child inched around his mother, peering up at him.

"This is Thomas. Say hi to Captain Wyatt."

"Hullo."

"Hey, sport."

Tina patted his head. "He misses his dad."

"I bet."

Kate looked at Rick for a long moment, and he felt she wanted to say something, her eyes were so sad just then. Instead she invited Tina into the living room.

Kate sat, nuzzling the infant, and Rick was riveted by the sight of her cuddling the tiny newborn.

"I'll leave you two ladies," he said, and went to the kitchen.

When Tina frowned, Kate said, "Kids scare him."

Then Thomas wiggled off the sofa and headed toward the kitchen. His mom started to call him back, but Kate stopped her. "If he can face armed rebels, he can face a four-year-old."

She wanted to go in there and watch him with the child, but she turned her attention back to her friend. Rick didn't want children. She did. With him. And even as they were patching up the holes in their marriage, she wondered if she'd ever be truly happy if being married to him kept her from her dream of having children of her own.

In the kitchen Rick sat in his chair, toying with the salt shaker. Seeing Kate with the baby made him want to see her hold his child. Which was stupid, since he'd never had a role model to help him be a father. He wouldn't make a good dad. He didn't even know how parents were supposed to behave.

Suddenly there was a little face beside him.

"Hi," a small voice said.

"Hello, Thomas."

"What are you doing?

"Eating lunch. Want some?"

"I had hamburgers. I get to have a lot of them when Dad's not here."

"How about dessert?"

"Whatcha got?"

What did they have? "Cookies?"

The boy shrugged and Rick stood. The boy barely came to his knees, for crying out loud. Rick bent, meeting his gaze at eye level. "Want to sit on the counter?"

"Really?"

Rick deposited the boy on the counter near the fridge. Then he poured a small glass of milk and brought over the cookie jar. The child seemed to inspect the contents for a lot longer than Rick thought was necessary before he selected one.

"Take two, they're free."

He giggled.

"My mom said you got hurt, huh?"

"Yes. I did."

"Shot with a bullet."

With a rifle, he thought, but didn't correct him. "Yes."

"Did it hurt?"

"Sure it did."

"Did it bleed?"

"Yes," Rick said, and wasn't sure how much a kid his age should know.

"Did you cry?"

"No."

"How come? I cry."

"Didn't matter. I was alone."

"Mom says just 'cuz you're a boy doesn't mean you can't cry."

"Your mom's right."

"So did you cry?"

Clearly he wasn't giving up on the subject. "No, I bit my tongue."

"Lemme see."

Rick showed him.

"I don't see nuthin'."

"See anything," Rick corrected, "and it's all better."

"Can I see the scar?"

"Why?"

The boy shrugged. Rick slipped his arm free of its sleeve and showed him.

"Is my dad gonna get one of those?"

Oh hell. "No, Thomas." He righted his shirt quickly. "I don't think so. Your father is smarter."

Thomas smiled. "Yeah, he is."

"Are you excited about seeing him?"

"He comes home in three days and a wake up."

Rick grinned. The military countdown. Kate once had a chart on the wall that had the Marine emblem divided like a puzzle. Each day she'd color in a numbered block. The "wake up" was when the day finally arrived.

"We're going to play games and eat pizza and all sorts of stuff."

The boy chatted fast and furiously, telling Rick everything he wanted to do with his dad. Rick leaned against the counter, watching the kid drink his milk and jam in the rest of the cookie. He took one for himself, asking Thomas a couple of questions. The kid was sharp, and talking with him was surprisingly easy.

When he looked up, Kate and Tina were standing in the doorway. Tina held the baby. Rick nudged the boy and he looked up.

"Uh-oh. I'm not supposed to be sitting on the counter."

"Yeah, me neither." Rick took the empty glass, then lifted the child down. "I think we're safe, pal," he said in a conspirital voice, glancing toward the boy. "They don't look mad."

Kate stared at Rick, unable to take her eyes off him and his ease with Thomas.

"We're leaving, Thomas," Tina said.

"Aw, man," the boy groused.

They saw Tina and her children to their car, Rick helping strap the boy in. Kate and Tina hugged, made vague plans to have lunch sometime after her husband came home.

"See you later, Capt'n," the boy said.

"Bye, Thomas. Watch your six."

The boy saluted him and Rick's smile widened. As the family drove off, Rick looked at Kate. "Sweet kid. Did you know he can read already?"

"Bet his father is proud of that."

"Yeah. Thomas talks a mile a minute. It's hard to keep track."

"Yes, they're like that. Everything is new and exciting to them."

Kate bit her lip to keep from blurting out her secret. Seeing Rick with the boy gave her a little twinge of hope, but then Thomas was another man's child, not theirs. Big difference.

"Kate? Something wrong?"

She glanced at Rick as they went back inside. "Why would you ask?"

"You look, I don't know…funny."

"I'm fine. How about a workout with weights?" she said, changing the subject.

Rick nodded, trying not to frown. He was more in tune with her emotions now and he knew there was something she wasn't saying. He almost dreaded hearing it, and decided to count his blessings and go with it till she was ready.

But suddenly it felt like a timed charge was about to go off between them.

On the flight line on the base, the crowd of people and the noise were almost smothering, an excited happiness permeating the air making everyone smile.

Kate glanced at her husband, standing proudly and looking sexy in his jungle uniform as he saluted Marines that passed him. Kate wondered for a second if he'd knock himself out with the cast. The airplane opened and Marines rushed across the deck to their families. She and Rick waited patiently amid the throngs of children running toward their fathers.

He smiled down at the kids. "You know, I used to look at your parents and think what a great childhood you must have had. I was almost jealous." Rick looked at Kate. "But I knew you loved me, and when you said you'd marry me I was glad I'd get to know your family."

"So you married me for my dad, huh?"

He chuckled. "My uncle didn't want a kid around. He was young, and being a surrogate father to a boy with a bad attitude wasn't easy for him. He didn't hit me or anything—I was bigger than him, in any case. But he just didn't care. Plus I don't think he liked his sister very much."

"So you were more or less on your own?"

"Yeah."

"You changed everything yourself."

Rick frowned at Kate, pouring himself a cup of coffee from the service set up for the troops and families.

"Look where you are now. A college graduate, a highly trained and decorated Marine commander. That was inside that boy all the time. So what pushed the unruly kid to make a change?"

"I guess it was Alice."

Kate arched a brow, looking a little jealous.

"My girl in high school. Her family didn't want us seeing each other, and looking back, if I were a dad, I wouldn't want her seeing me, either." He frowned. "I was hotheaded and reckless. So they forbade her to see me. We toughed it out for a bit, then she went with some ball player."

Kate nudged him to go on as they strolled the circumference of the flight deck, away from the troops still unloading from the plane.

"I hated it, that my looks and attitude marked me as trouble in sneakers. So I studied. I didn't do much else except work a weekend job."

He'd earned scholarships with his grades and had been selected for a free ride to the Naval Academy. He'd told her about his life in college, but not much before that.

"You said once that you fit in right away at the academy. That it was like a family."

"I knew someone there actually gave a damn."

"Someone here does, too."

"Ah, baby, I know." He slung his arm about her. He looked around and, surrounded by these families, soaked up the scene.

"So what about this woman you told about your childhood? Why did she turn and run?"

"Hell if I know. I didn't expect it, that's for sure. She wanted someone with a..." He stopped, thinking.

"A pleasant uneventful childhood," Kate suggested, and he nodded. "Oh, for the love of Mike, like that makes a difference? Who's childhood is pure? What a horrible, self-centered—"

Rick could tell she was getting mad on his behalf, and he smiled widely. She clamped her lips shut, laughing at herself.

"Her loss," she said with feeling. "I don't see how she could have resisted you. You were too intense to ignore, so passionate about your devotion, your duty, your men. I admired that. Even the way you went after me."

"I thought I'd scare you off."

"You said as much. You used to hold my hand as if you wanted to. Not to make a pass."

He took her hand now. "I was trying *to* make a pass."

She nudged him and walked back toward the crowd. "When my dad first met you he said, 'Grass doesn't grow under that man's feet, lass. Marry him fast.'"

Rick felt the warmth of pride. Her dad was a fine man. "We used to have some great talks."

"Lectures."

"To *you,* maybe. Not me."

"My Da has a glib Irish tongue. He was lecturing you, you just didn't know it." A silence stretched, and Kate said, "Why couldn't you tell me this before?"

"I thought…well no, I didn't think. Strong and silent seemed better than unloading because of the last time I told—" He stopped abruptly and looked at Kate. "I didn't want to see pity in your eyes."

"So what do you see now?"

"That you're…" he searched her face, searched for the words "…in my soul."

Kate felt something move through her, straight into her heart like an arrow. She loved this new man who was emerging. She touched his jaw and curled her fingers around the back of his neck. "No public displays of affection?" she said, a breath away from his mouth.

"Risk it, please."

She laughed against his lips, then kissed him, and he drew her to his length. He wanted more, wanted her alone again. Then he heard his name being called.

Rick looked up, easing back. Jace was gesturing to them and together they met with his troops. Kate listened as Rick spoke frankly with his men, then thanked the corpsman who'd saved his life. The shock on their faces when Rick spoke so openly about his feelings was enough to boost Kate's spirits. She didn't mind being pushed aside. There was a bond between these men a wife would never understand.

Kelly stepped up beside her, offering her coffee from a thick paper cup. The sounds of laughter and babies crying, some being held by their fathers for the first time, filled the air around them.

"He seems different, Kate."

"Really? You think?" She didn't know anyone else had noticed.

"Oh, honey, give yourself a break, will you? You can't change this part of them, but the time at home— that's your business."

She glanced at the Sergeant Major's wife. "You knew."

"What battalion doesn't know everything?"

Kate groaned. "Yeah, I guess. He had the nerve to say the men don't talk."

They laughed over that bit of garbage.

"I'm glad to see you helping him with this."

"He needed a watchdog."

"I'd say he's the watchdog right now."

Kate's gaze was on Rick as he glanced over the crowd. She was almost breathless as she waited until he found her. Then his gaze locked on her like radar, and her heart gave a little skip. She hoped that sudden feeling of excitement never went away. Then he simply held his hand out to her. She excused herself and went to him. That gesture, him wanting her near, told her that Rick *was* different now. Whether it was his wound, the threat to his life or her, she didn't know, nor did she care.

After an hour and some motivating speeches from the battalion commanding officer, the crowd thinned, the families eager to bring their Marines home. Rick was in the passenger seat as Kate drove off the base.

"They did well, really well."

"You trained them."

"Ha, the Gunnery Sergeants did."

He stared out the window at the passing scenery, noticing the banners on the fences declaring love and welcoming the troops home.

"I've got the best troops," he said. "God knows I'm tested just as much as they are."

"What do you mean?"

"My judgment is," he explained. "I have to stay so focused, so objective, and give orders without emotion, but knowing them and their families as I do, it's tough. I could be ordering them to die."

"I know what you mean."

He looked at her, a little skeptical, and she shrugged. "Well, it's sorta like in the O.R. or the emergency room. One mistake and, well, same thing. I have to trust my training, though it's not the same as battle, of course. I do get a little too involved with my patients. But that lack of emotion is what makes you a good leader."

Rick flushed, then reached for her hand. "I'd rather be a good husband."

She sent him a sexy smile full of promise. "Are we home yet?"

"Drive faster."

Rick slid his hand over her thigh, under her skirt. She wriggled in the car seat, speeding, then slowing down. "Stop! This is dangerous."

"I want you."

Her entire body clenched like an unsprung coil. Rick kept talking, telling her what he would do to her once they were in their bedroom. Kate's breath came in tight gasps, and when his hand moved higher, a fingertip stroking her, she thought she'd spin the car out of control.

"Rick. Please."

"Oh, yeah, I plan to."

"I mean—"

"I know exactly what you mean."

She turned down their street, careful of the kids playing, and pulled into the drive. Rick was out of the car and beside her door before she could collect herself. He grabbed her hand, unlocking the house and pulling her inside.

She dropped her purse, then was in his arms, kissing him. "We've made a spectacle for the neighbors. I heard Candice next door laughing."

"Ask me if I care," he said, walking her backward,

unbuttoning her blouse as he did. He worked it off, flinging it aside.

Kate felt giddy, so like a teenager, as if they were getting away with something they shouldn't. When they reached the bedroom, her _____ somewhere in the hall with her shoes. H_____ against the bed, falling on the mattress _____ with him. His hand cupped her behind and she started on the thick buttons of his heavy camouflage shirt. He rose up just enough for her to peel it off him.

Then he smiled, sliding his fingers inside her panties. "I love these little lacy things."

"I know." She yanked the green T-shirt over his head, then kissed him.

Rick felt torn apart, her kiss was so eager, so strong, so devouring and erotic.

"Hurry, Rick, please." She was suddenly wild, desperate, and he responded, loving that she was showering this on him.

"Rip them," she said into his ear, sending chills down his body.

He yanked and the thin material shredded in his fist. Then his trousers were open, her hand stroking him. "In a hurry?" he murmured.

"Oh, yes, I don't know why, but yes!"

He rolled her to her back, spreading her thighs, then pushed inside her in one hard stroke.

"Oh, Kate," he groaned.

She whimpered beneath him, thrusting her hips forward, and he understood what she wanted, needed.

Fast, hot and right now. Rick obeyed, making love to her, experiencing the tidal wave of passion as it roared to life and raced toward the explosions.

Then it happened, taking them by surprise, and Rick realized they weren't using protection. And in his heart, he didn't care.

Ten

Rick watched the corpsman cut off the cast. "God, I've been looking forward to this for so damn long."

The doctor stood by, making notes in the chart as the corpsman worked. "You'll be ready to return to duty in a couple weeks but you're not to use the arm to lift anything more than a coffee cup till I give the go-ahead, Captain. It stays in the sling."

"I can live with that." He'd been doing weeks of physical therapy since the first bandages had come off, and he was ready to dump the cast and get back in uniform. Back to work.

"Do I need to give the orders to your wife?" The doctor flashed a cheeky grin.

"She'll demand them, anyway."

"I'm not surprised." The doctor set aside the chart and manipulated Rick's wrist and shoulder. "A woman who flies to Germany to meet the medical plane is not a woman I'd want to argue with."

Rick's head jerked up, his features taut. "I beg your pardon?"

The doctor looked uncomfortable for a moment, then sighed. "She met the plane from Kandahar, Captain. She was outside the O.R. during surgery and by your side till you woke from recovery."

Rick scowled, glancing at the door and knowing Kate was on the other side.

"She never mentioned it to you?"

"No, sir."

"I'm not surprised. She asked us not to tell you. I didn't question it. I figured she had her reasons, but I thought you should know what kind of woman you have for a wife."

For a brief moment, Rick wondered why she hadn't told him. Then he realized that when he hadn't gone after her when she'd left, she'd thought he didn't want her in his life.

"Thanks for telling me, sir. Don't let on that I know, okay?"

The doctor nodded and the corpsman helped Rick into the sling.

He'd keep this secret to himself for now.

It proved a couple things: that she hadn't come to help him out of pity or obligation, and that all he'd really had to do to bring her back was reach out.

When he flung open the door, she smiled and rose from her chair. And he and the doctor exchanged an amused glance when she asked for his prognosis and instructions. For once, Rick was damn glad she was a pill about it, and just accepted that his wife was a perfectionist.

Yeah, he thought. He could live with that.

It was an impromptu surprise for Rick. He didn't know the wives of his staff NCOs had called ahead. Let him think the parade of friends and food was spontaneous, Kate thought. The house and yard she still thought of as hers was filled with people again. There had been lots of welcome-home parties. Some private, some not, but seeing her loved ones again was like renewing a part of herself she'd lost when she left.

Kate ignored the regret that buffeted her, and brought a tray out to the porch, then went into the yard, where Rick was grilling burgers on the barbecue. A couple of wives were in the pool with the kids, and Kate was refreshing drinks and beers when she heard Jace.

"I'll take that bet."

She glanced at the lieutenant. "What bet is that?" She handed him a fresh beer.

"The baby pool. You know, how many deployment babies we get by next rotation. Can't collect for at least five months, though, when the girls start to show, but I have odds on at least ten babies."

"And you think it's not *planned?*" Kate said. But it happened so much that when the troops returned, there were a lot of surprise deployment pregnancies. Kate kept her features impassive as she thought that she'd been one of them. She'd gotten pregnant just before Rick left for six months.

"I lost last time," Staff Sergeant Ridge said. "And I'm glad." He glanced over at Tina, who was holding Emma's feet in the water, and winked at her. Thomas, not to be left out, rushed to his dad, and his father scooped him up, wet bathing suit and all.

"You going to be part of the pool odds, ma'am?" Ridge asked.

"No, not this time around," Kate replied, trying to keep the pain out of her voice.

Over the grill top, Rick met Kate's gaze. She could tell by his expression he was thinking of the line he'd drawn between them because he didn't want kids.

"I don't know about that," he said, and her brows shot up. The shock on her face was readable to anyone, even Thomas. Rick put out his hand, keeping the boy back from the grill. "What would you like, Thomas?" he asked quickly, wondering why he'd opened that door. "Hot dogs, hamburgers?"

Kate turned away, feeling the euphoria of the past few days slipping away as she brought drinks to her girlfriends, then eagerly took baby Emma from Tina so she could have a break. Dan came to his wife, sliding into the water with his son to play while Kate nestled under the umbrellas with the infant. She chatted with the baby, who didn't know her voice from Adam's, and her throat tightened as the child latched on to her little finger.

How could Rick not want this? she thought, and kissed Emma's downy hair. She lifted her gaze.

He was watching her, the grill smoking, and he didn't take his eyes off her until Jace nudged him to pay attention.

Rick flipped the burgers, laying some on a platter, but seeing Kate again with the baby struck him like a slap. He felt as if he were cheating her out of something wonderful. All he had to do was look at her face and see how much she wanted a baby.

His baby.

His. The words kept repeating in his mind and a strange feeling made his skin chill. "Jace, you ever wonder if you'd make a good father?"

"No, not really. I haven't found Miss Right yet. And I'd like to have her alone for a while first."

"But if you did."

Jace frowned and Rick wasn't sure he should get into this conversation right now.

"I think I'd be a good dad, yeah. My dad was great. But I don't think that has anything to do with it. You have to want to be a father, and want to be able to change your life for them." Jace glanced at the kids whooping it up in the pool. "They're pretty easy to please. I'd just want to be sure, though. It's not like you can give them back, you know."

Rick dragged his gaze from Kate and smiled. "I can't picture you a father."

"I can picture you, though."

Rick's head snapped up. "Why?"

"You're fair with the men, you give them all equal respect. You know their families, you consider their lives and troubles."

"That's my job."

"Hey, the younger men idolize you, Rick. And I've had other commanders, believe me. They weren't as attentive or considerate."

Rick shut off the grill and called out that chow was hot and ready. Kate rose and moved close, handing out towels, and Rick swept his arm around her, his gaze on the little girl all in pink. Emma fussed, and Kate lifted her to her shoulder. The little girl looked up at Rick with that wide-eyed innocence he found so rare, and he felt as if he were drowning.

To be responsible for someone so small, he thought. Kids depended on you for everything. Did Kate want a baby for them or because she wanted to feel needed?

"Why do you want one, Kate?"

She turned, her eyes locked with his. "Because our baby will be a part of us both. Our future. And don't tease me like that again."

He heard the bite in her tone. "Who said I was teasing?"

Kate moved away, angered that he'd dangle the promise of a child in front of her like that.

The doctors Kate worked for called her to assist in surgery, and she went, needing to be out of the house. Being around Rick twenty-four hours a day was great, but she'd been away for two months now and needed to return to her job, needed to reestablish the connections. Or lose her seniority. Aside from that there was only so much house cleaning and errands she could do without going crazy and feeling a little useless.

Rick didn't mind, promising to not do any handsprings in the backyard. He was healing faster, his strength returning with therapy and weight training. He'd even gone into work for a couple of hours.

They'd talked more in the last weeks than they ever had, and Kate felt the solidity of their marriage had grown. It was she who was keeping them apart.

She knew she should tell him, and as she passed the nursery on the maternity ward, she felt the pangs she'd pushed aside for years now.

For Rick.

How was she supposed to convince her own husband that she wanted to have his baby, without sending him off in the other direction? How was she going to tell him she'd been pregnant once before? She'd tried twice since the party and couldn't muster the nerve, not when he looked so happy and contented. It wouldn't be long before he sensed something was up and turned the tables on her.

Kate dreaded it. It didn't take long for a powder keg to go up in smoke.

Rick tossed the rubber ball, catching it, then flung it up behind his back and caught it again. Kate was at work for a few hours, which was good. Aside from the fact that she was getting cabin fever, she'd yell at him for this. He worked with a hand vise and could crush a tomato with two fingers, but that wasn't how you handled explosives.

He didn't hear Kate come in the house.

She stepped into the kitchen, watching Rick juggle fruit in the air like a circus performer. "Well, I see you've been up to no good."

He spun around, looking so guilty she almost smiled. Fruit hit the floor and rolled under the table.

"Why didn't you tell me?"

"I was hoping it would be a surprise."

"It is. You don't need my help if you're that strong again."

Panic shot through him. Did she really think he

wanted her here just for physical therapy and sex? "I'm not one hundred percent. This is just dexterity."

"Fine."

Rick scowled, scooping up the fruit as he came to her. "Something's been bothering you lately. What is it?"

Kate let out a long-suffering breath. "We might be talking more, and God knows making love is incredible, but today I realized again that we still don't want the same things."

A chill wrenched though him. "Whoa. What brought that on?"

"I was in the maternity ward."

"Oh."

"It wasn't just that. Do you know how hurt I was when Ridge asked if we were going to have a child and you said, 'I don't know about that'?"

"Yes, I think I do."

"No, you don't. It hurt, Rick. Because I know you don't want kids. It hurts even more because—" she met his gaze and sucked in a breath "—I was pregnant with your baby."

He went pale. "Oh, God." Rick did the math, and since she wasn't presenting him with a child, he understood. "You miscarried."

"Yes."

"You didn't bother to tell me? Talk about me shutting *you* out, Kate."

"Don't even start, Rick. I tried to tell you. You were

on some mission and couldn't be reached. Ask your Major. I tried. But it was classified."

He thought back and knew she was right. "Why didn't you tell me when I came back?"

"Why? I'd already lost the baby, and telling you would have just made things worse. What was the point?"

"I had a right to know."

"Really? You didn't want babies with me. You didn't even come after me. What was I supposed to think? A baby would have made you feel obligated."

The last word came out like a curse, and Rick winced.

"I didn't want you that way and I still don't."

"And if you're pregnant now?"

Kate inhaled, her look so frantic and lost that Rick stepped toward her. She backed away. "I'm not. I'd know, so don't dangle a 'maybe baby' in front of me, Rick. It hurts."

"Who said I was? I've been thinking about it a lot."

"Why?"

"You want a child."

She shook her head. "It has to be mutual. I want to have *your* baby." She said the words around the knot in her throat. "Not any child."

"What do you want from me?"

She lifted her gaze, tears spilling. "I want my husband to love me enough to want roots with me. To make the family you never had." She took a breath. "You would want that, too, if you'd just let yourself believe you're capable. I think you'd make the best father in the world because you wouldn't neglect your child. You would never do what happened to you."

"Kate, honey, I don't have any experience—"

"Neither do I! Who really does? I was willing to take a chance on us. Wanting a family is saying what I've been trying to tell you for years—that I'll never stop loving you. I'm not going anywhere."

"But you did."

"Yes, so you'd come after me, show me you loved me."

Rick scraped a hand over his short hair and cursed. "I didn't think you loved me enough to stick around."

"Oh, Rick."

He gathered her close, holding her. "If I don't agree to babies, you'll be gone?" He held his breath.

"No, of course not." *He's still afraid,* she thought.

"But you won't be happy."

"Yes, we will," she said bravely, "and that means more to me than children." Kate choked on her tears, pushing out of his arms and rushing from the room.

Rick dropped into a chair, his head in his hands, wondering how he could screw up a good thing so fast.

They walked on pins and needles.

Rick could kick himself for not being careful when he spoke. Kate wasn't mad, she wasn't sullen, she was her same old self. But he knew what was beneath, and it wasn't the woman he'd been falling in love with again for the past two months.

"Kate," he said, walking into the living room.

She was curled on the sofa, reading a novel.

"We need to talk."

She set the book down, inviting him to join her. Her smile was forced, but so pretty his heart ached. "I'm sorry you had to suffer alone. Losing a baby couldn't have been easy."

Kate looked away, remembering. "I felt so alone and scared. Then when it was over, I felt just…empty."

Rick grasped her hand. "That's how I felt when you were gone. Hell, every time we're apart." He struggled for a second, then blurted, "I'm scared."

"Of kids? I know."

He shook his head. "No, not because of the responsibility, or whether I'd make a good father or not. I think I would, actually, but I'm terrified of leaving you alone with a child."

"Because you were shot?"

He nodded.

"If it happened, I could handle it."

"I know you could, but I wouldn't want our child to have to grow up without a father."

She blinked. *Our child?* Was he really coming around? She wouldn't get her hopes up. "But they'd have a mother. I understand your feelings, Rick. It will take me a little bit to accept it in here." She touched her heart. "I already knew it in here when I married you." She tapped her temple.

"No, baby, you're stronger than I thought, and what I mean is I—" The phone rang, cutting him off, and Rick cursed under his breath, then grabbed it up. "Yes, sir." He frowned at Kate. "With my wife, sir? Yes, sir." Rick hung up. "The C.O. wants me at the base with you. In twenty minutes."

Kate hopped off the sofa and dashed into the guest room. Rick had a quick shower and shave, and found his uniform laid out. He could still smell her perfume in the air. It made his arms ache for her.

Kate waited by the door, checking her appearance in the hall mirror when Rick's image appeared behind her. She turned, her heartbeat tripping a little. "Feel good to be without the cast?"

She tried to smile. It didn't quite reach her eyes and it hurt Rick to see it. "Yes, it does."

She handed him the car keys. "I think you're well enough to drive." She turned away and he felt the chill in her tone. As if she were leaving him, though she was still here.

At the car Rick grasped her arm gently and she lifted her gaze. Her eyes were glossy and Rick groaned. "Honey, talk to me. We can't go on like this."

"I know, we'll talk. But duty is calling."

They got into the car and Rick started the engine. They made idle talk till they reached battalion headquarters.

"Rick? Look." She pointed to the men in formation. Rick parked and got out, but a Marine rushed to open Kate's door before he could, then escorted her to a

small covered area filled with chairs. She frowned at
her friends there, at the C.O.s and Sergeant Major's
wives, then looked out on the parade. The battalion
was stretched out over the length of a football field.

Rick was ordered to report to his C.O. When he
stopped in front of the Colonel and saluted, the
Colonel returned the salute. Then a voice over a loud-
speaker called attention to orders. The entire battalion
snapped from parade rest to attention.

As Rick stared straight ahead, he could see Kate in
his line of vision. He listened to the citation for brav-
ery, then the awarding of a Purple Heart—to him.

All Rick thought of was Kate.

As the account of the attack was recited, his commander pinned the medal—a purple heart with George
Washington's silhouette in gold in the center—to his
uniform. Then the band struck up the "Marine's Hymn,"
and the men were dismissed. Troops converged on Rick.

Kate stood with her friends, tears in her eyes. She
was so proud of him, of his survival, of how much
they'd grown in the past months. She could live with
the love of her life. She could accept that kids weren't
in the cards for them, perhaps until much later. And she
wanted to tell him that.

Rick instantly missed her presence and after shaking hands with several comrades and well-wishers, he
excused himself from the conversation that normally
got his blood pumping. He found her surrounded by
other wives.

Rick murmured, "Excuse me, ladies," as he made his way among them. "I need to speak to my wife."

"Rick, what is it?"

He gripped her arms, planting a strong quick kiss on her lips. "Don't give up on me."

"What?" She glanced around at the others, her face flushing.

"In the past couple of months I've learned a lot about myself, and you, but I'm still learning." To her astonishment he removed his Purple Heart, slipping his fingers inside her blouse to pin it on her.

Kate looked from the pin to him and back. "What are you doing? It's yours!"

"No honey, it's yours."

"I didn't earn it."

"Yes, you did. I might have been shot, but there are all kinds of wounds." She softened, staring up at him. "You're the one who braved mine. You're the one who faced an opponent." He gazed tenderly at her. "You healed more than my shoulder."

Kate swallowed. A small crowd listened to his words, but she hung on each one, the onlookers fading away.

"I've been alone all my life and when I found you I stopped looking."

"Oh, Rick." She couldn't get past the knot in her throat, resting her hands on his arms as he pulled her close.

"When you walked through our front door, I was

angry and yet so happy that I could breathe again. You're my air, my life. You're the reason I fought death in the field. The reason I wanted to *live*." He cleared his throat, his every emotion sharp and bright in his eyes. "You rescued me from a place I didn't know I was hiding in, and now that I'm out of there, I want to make roots with you." He leaned closer, his eyes dark with promise as he whispered, "And babies with you."

Kate choked on her breath. She didn't expect him to change overnight, but that he'd opened the door made her deliriously happy. "I love you so much, you know that?"

"Yes, I do. You flew all the way to Germany for me, didn't you?"

She blinked, then her smile widened. "Doctors can't be trusted with secrets."

"No more secrets. We say what we mean." Rick fished in his pocket, then took her hand. "I love you, Kate. I love you more now than the first time I put these on you."

He slid her wedding rings back on her finger. The clear white stones sparkled in the morning light as the crowd around them roared with Oh-rah and applause.

"Me, too, Rick. Always, always."

He grinned, the dazzling smile surprising some people, but not Kate. She knew him better than he did himself. In or out of uniform, Rick was still intense and powerful.

And the love of her life.

* * * * *

Silhouette® Desire®

Coming in March 2005
from Silhouette Desire

The next installment in

DYNASTIES: THE ASHTONS

SOCIETY-PAGE SEDUCTION
by Maureen Child
(SD #1639)

When dashingly handsome billionaire
Simon Pearce was deserted at the altar,
wedding planner Megan Ashton filled in for the
bride. Before long, their faux romance turned into
scorching passion. Yet little did Simon know Megan
had not only sparked excitement between his
sheets, she'd also brought scandal to his door....

Available at your favorite retail outlet.

Silhouette
Desire

From *USA TODAY* bestselling author

Cait London

TOTAL PACKAGE

The latest book in her sizzling miniseries,
HEARTBREAKERS, featuring the delicious
men of the Stepanov family and the
passionate women they're drawn to.

HEART BREAKERS

Photographer Sidney Blakely
comes to Amoteh for a
photo shoot after being
jilted by a longtime love for
a more "wifely" woman. But
Danya Stepanov senses the
hot blood that runs through
her veins and knows he's
just the man to bring it
to a boil....

*Available at
your favorite retail outlet.*

Only from Silhouette Books!

If you enjoyed what you just read,
then we've got an offer you can't resist!

Take 2 bestselling
love stories FREE!
Plus get a FREE surprise gift!

Clip this page and mail it to Silhouette Reader Service™

IN U.S.A.	IN CANADA
3010 Walden Ave.	P.O. Box 609
P.O. Box 1867	Fort Erie, Ontario
Buffalo, N.Y. 14240-1867	L2A 5X3

YES! Please send me 2 free Silhouette Desire® novels and my free surprise gift. After receiving them, if I don't wish to receive anymore, I can return the shipping statement marked cancel. If I don't cancel, I will receive 6 brand-new novels every month, before they're available in stores! In the U.S.A., bill me at the bargain price of $3.80 plus 25¢ shipping and handling per book and applicable sales tax, if any*. In Canada, bill me at the bargain price of $4.47 plus 25¢ shipping and handling per book and applicable taxes**. That's the complete price and a savings of at least 10% off the cover prices—what a great deal! I understand that accepting the 2 free books and gift places me under no obligation ever to buy any books. I can always return a shipment and cancel at any time. Even if I never buy another book from Silhouette, the 2 free books and gift are mine to keep forever.

225 SDN DZ9F
326 SDN DZ9G

Name	(PLEASE PRINT)	
Address	Apt.#	
City	State/Prov.	Zip/Postal Code

Not valid to current Silhouette Desire® subscribers.

Want to try two free books from another series?
Call 1-800-873-8635 or visit www.morefreebooks.com.

* Terms and prices subject to change without notice. Sales tax applicable in N.Y.
** Canadian residents will be charged applicable provincial taxes and GST.
   All orders subject to approval. Offer limited to one per household.
   ® are registered trademarks owned and used by the trademark owner and or its licensee.

DES04R   ©2004 Harlequin Enterprises Limited

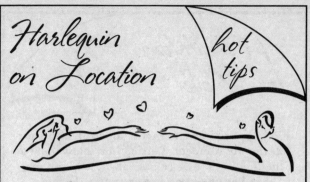

Harlequin on Location

hot tips

Wherever your dream date location,
pick a setting and a time that won't be
interrupted by your daily responsibilities.
This is a special time together. Here are
a few hopelessly romantic settings to
inspire you—they might as well be ripped
right out of a Harlequin romance novel!

Bad weather can be so good.

Take a walk together after a fresh snowfall or when it's just stopped raining. Pick a snowball (or a puddle) fight, and see how long it takes to get each other soaked to the bone. Then enjoy drying off in front of a fire, or perhaps surrounded by lots and lots of candles with yummy hot chocolate to warm things up.

Candlelight dinner for two…in the bedroom.

Romantic music and candles will instantly transform the place you sleep into a cozy little love nest, perfect for nibbling. Why not lay down a blanket and open a picnic basket at the foot of your bed? Or set a beautiful table with your finest dishes and glowing candles to set the mood. Either way, a little bubbly and lots of light finger foods will make this a meal to remember.

A Wild and Crazy Weeknight.

Do something unpredictable…on a weeknight straight from work. Go to an art opening, a farm-team baseball game, the local playhouse, a book signing by an author or a jazz club—anything but the humdrum blockbuster movie. There's something very romantic about being a little wild and crazy—or at least out of the ordinary—that will bring out the flirt in both of you. And you won't be able to resist thinking about each other in anticipation of your hot date…or telling everyone the day after.

An Invitation for Love

hot tips

Find a special way to invite your guy into your Harlequin Moment. Letting him know you're looking for a little romance will help put his mind on the same page as yours. In fact, if you do it right, he won't be able to stop thinking about you until he sees you again!

Send him a long-stemmed rose tied to an invitation that leaves a lot up to the imagination.

Autograph a favorite photo of you and tape it on the appointed day in his day planner. Block out the hours he'll be spending with you.

Send him a local map and put an *X* on the place you want him to meet you. Write: "I'm lost without you. Come find me. Tonight at 8." Use magazine cutouts and photographs to paste images of romance and the two of you all over the map.

Send him something personal that he'll recognize as yours to his office. Write: "If found, please return. Owner offers reward to anyone returning item by 7:30 on Saturday night." Don't sign the card.

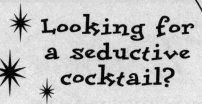

Looking for a seductive cocktail?

hot tips

Try *Ero-Desiac*—
a dazzling martini

With its warm apricot walls yet cool atmosphere, Verlaine is quickly becoming one of New York's hottest nightspots. Verlaine created a light, subtle yet seductive martini for Harlequin: the Ero-Desiac. Sake warms the heart and soul, while jasmine and passion fruit ignite the senses....

The Ero-Desiac

Combine vodka, sake, passion fruit puree and jasmine tea. Mix and shake. Strain into a martini glass, then rest pomegranate syrup on the edge of the martini glass and drizzle the syrup down the inside of the glass.

COMING NEXT MONTH

#1639 SOCIETY-PAGE SEDUCTION—Maureen Child
Dynasties: The Ashtons
When dashingly handsome billionaire Simon Pearce was deserted at the altar, wedding planner Megan Ashton filled in for the bride. Before long, their faux romance turned into scorching passion. Yet little did Simon know Megan had not only sparked excitement between his sheets, she'd also brought scandal to his door....

#1640 A MAN APART—Joan Hohl
The moment rancher Justin Grainger laid eyes on sexy Hannah Deturk, he vowed not to leave town without getting into her bed. Their whirlwind affair left them both wanting more. But Hannah feared falling for a loner like Justin could only mean heartache...unless she convinced him to be a man apart no longer.

#1641 HER *FIFTH* HUSBAND?—Dixie Browning
Divas Who Dish
She had a gift for picking the wrong men...her four failed marriages were a testament to her lousy judgment. So when interior designer Sasha Lasiter met stunningly sexy John Batchelor Smith she fervently fought their mutual attraction. But John was convinced Sasha's fifth time would be the charm—only if he was the groom!

#1642 TOTAL PACKAGE—Cait London
Heartbreakers
After being dumped by her longtime love, photographer Sidney Blakely met the total package in smart, and devastatingly handsome Danya Stepanov. Before long he had Sidney spoiled rotten, but she couldn't help wondering whether this red-hot relationship could survive her demanding career.

#1643 UNDER THE TYCOON'S PROTECTION—Anna DePalo
Her life was in danger, but the last person proud Allison Whittaker wanted to protect her was her old crush, bodyguard Connor Rafferty. Having been betrayed by Connor before, Allison still burned with anger, but close quarters rekindled the fiery desire that raged between them...and ignited deeper emotions that put her heart in double jeopardy.

#1644 HIGH-STAKES PASSION—Juliet Burns
Ever since his career-ending injury, ex-rodeo champion Mark Malone walked around with a chip on his shoulder. Housekeeper Aubrey Tyson arranged a high-stakes game of poker to lighten this sexy cowboy's mood—but depending on the luck of the draw, she could wind up in his bed...!

SDCNM0205